SHARON KENNEDY HARRISON

FRAUDULENT
JUSTICE

Trilogy Christian Publishers

A Wholly Owned Subsidiary of Trinity Broadcasting Network

2442 Michelle Drive

Tustin, CA 92780

10 9 8 7 6 5 4 3 2 1

Library of Congress Cataloging-in-Publication Data is available.

ISBN 979-8-89333-032-8

ISBN 979-8-89333-033-5 (ebook)

ACKNOWLEDGMENTS

Thanks to my family and friends for their help and support in writing this book. In the beginning, it seemed like a daunting task. But with their encouragement, it finally came to fruition. It has been a joy and quite gratifying to complete this endeavor.

Now to Him who is able to do immeasurably more than all we ask or imagine, according to His power that is at work within us, to Him be glory... (Ephesians 3: 20).

TABLE OF CONTENTS

CHAPTER 1

He was ready to leave, and he'd had enough. He'd played the fool one time too many. Having a shattered heart was not the way he was going to live again. What would he do now? *Carrie thought she knew me, but she was wrong. She never truly loved me like I thought.* Who was she? How had he let his heart be so vulnerable? Her blue eyes and long blonde hair had caught him off guard. Her beautiful, shy, but seductive smile had made him feel like he was the only person in the room. He fell for her from the first minute he saw her. Hard. Love at first sight. But now, he knew that was just her way of seducing him. Her friend had told her about him, but he was unaware of it. He thought it was an accidental meeting.

Carrie McLan knew he was someone she wanted to meet so she set up an impromptu meeting, unbeknownst to him. He fell for her, hook, line, and sinker. He was a good catch for Carrie. Standing six feet two inches, muscular, broad shoulders, athletic looking, with blondish brown hair and a scruffy beard, Brock Morgan was handsome, and she was attracted to him. He had a degree in business and was motivated to succeed. Brock was well-trained in medical sales and brought in almost a six-figure income.

Carrie realized when she found out his salary that Brock could support her the way she deserved. She had her eyes set on living the good life, and Brock certainly could provide that for her. She was accustomed to having what she wanted. She didn't go to college like she had intended. She had gotten a good job out of high school and had various on-the-job training classes for advancement to boost her income. Her employer thought Carrie was a good prospect for the company because of her eagerness to learn. Her drive for success and money was what made her tick. She bought whatever she wanted. It didn't matter to her if she ran up the balance on her charge cards. She was tired of living the underprivileged life. Coming from what she considered to be a low-income family, she was determined to get out of the rut her parents seemed to be living in. From Carrie's point of view, they were satisfied with their lifestyle, content with living in mediocrity. She wanted more. All she needed to do was find someone to marry that could support her. She needed someone to love her and take care of her the way she wanted and deserved.

However, she required a lot of Brock's time. She was calling him all the time and needing him at every turn. Every whim she had, she called him. That was flattering at first. She made him feel needed. He liked helping people, and she always seemed to need help with something. Then he realized his business was failing. He'd lost his focus and his direction, all because he was caught up in her world. That's the last time he would get involved with a self-absorbed woman. He was frustrated. While he was thinking things over and reflecting on his life with Carrie, Brock finally realized that his friends had tried to warn him. When did he become so blind? He thought he was in love. His friends were just being overly dramatic, maybe even jealous, he told himself. 'She was a gold-digger,' they'd said, but he didn't listen. *We had so much fun together and great conversations*, he thought. *She told me she loved me. I thought I knew her like no one else. Then, I found out the truth.* Grief had taken a toll on him. How could he have been so blind? Was he that naïve, or was she just that good at lying? Brock kept beating himself up, but he knew it was time to stop. He had to get back in the game. He would lay the past aside; start over in a new town and with new friends. After turning in his resignation from his job, he could move on. Financially he was all right. He had excellent investments and a good savings account.

Brock was investigating new cities to move to on the internet, as he took some time to rest and pack. He went to the local big box store to buy moving supplies. Nashville seemed like as good a town as any. He knew some people who had vacationed there. They liked it, and he'd visited there when he was a teenager. When he got home, he ordered a pizza and began packing. It took a few days to wrap things up, but he was ready. Everything he owned was packed in his car and trailer. He drove from Pennsylvania, over a twelve-hour trip, where he would have some time to think and begin refocusing his life. All that mattered now was his career. Relationships weren't worth the risk.

CHAPTER 2

Waiting outside Brock's apartment building, acting like she was searching for her key, Carrie had to sneak in when a resident left. Going to Brock's apartment was the last thing she wanted to do, but she was desperate. She knocked. No answer.

"Come on Brock, let me in. We need to talk. I'm sorry for what I did. It was a foolish mistake." *Why doesn't he come to the door*, she thought anxiously.

She pounded on the door again, but he didn't answer. She decided to wait a few minutes to see if he'd come to the door or come home if he was gone. He didn't. As she started to leave, she spotted the maintenance man. *Maybe he'll know something*, she thought.

"Hi George, I was looking for Brock, I assumed he'd be here, but he's not answering the door."

"Left town!"

"What do you mean, he left?" she asked George.

"No, he couldn't have left town without telling me or saying goodbye," Carrie mumbled under her breath.

"Did he leave a forwarding address? Surely, he must have said something to you when he was leaving," Carrie said.

"No, ma'am. He just said he was leaving town and wouldn't be back. Needed a fresh start or something like that. I told him I'd miss him. He'd been really nice to me. He told me to take care of myself, and then he handed me $200. He told me to take my wife out for a nice dinner. Nice guy. I'm really going to miss him."

Carrie didn't say goodbye, she stomped her foot angrily, turned around and left. She had to find him.

CHAPTER 3

In route to Nashville, Brock took a few scenic detours to break up the monotony of the trip. Arriving in Nashville a couple of hours later than he'd anticipated, he checked into a major hotel chain. He needed a good bed, and this hotel had the best. He was exhausted after the long drive, but was hungry, so he decided to eat something, take a shower, and go to bed. He called the front desk to see where he could get the best pizza to have it delivered. By the time he took his shower and got his t-shirt and sweats on, the pizza was delivered to the front desk. Since he had already paid for it online, they brought it to his room. He ate the large pepperoni and mushroom pizza, listened to the local news, and turned in for the night.

He woke up at nearly 9:00 a.m. and sleeping in was nice and much needed. Brock ate breakfast at the hotel restaurant then decided to book a massage to alleviate the stress of the trip. Needing a double espresso, after the long trek yesterday, he went to a local coffee house a few blocks away that he'd passed coming into town. Getting another cup of coffee to go, he decided to go back to the hotel, take a swim in their pool, relax with the massage he'd booked before he left, and then later check out jobs on the internet. Arriving at his hotel room, he turned on the TV to check out the local news and weather while he was getting ready for his swim. After three hours of mindless activity, he got a late lunch and went back to his room. Turning on his computer, he searched the most prominent job websites. After perusing the jobs available, Brock sent in a few résumés. Before he left Pennsylvania, he made sure his résumé was up to date so he would be ready to send it out when he got to Nashville. He decided to chill out awhile, take a nap, then drove around a little to get his bearings before going back to the fitness room at the hotel. The next morning, he decided to call a company that looked appealing. He landed an interview for the next day with one of the top executives at the company. That seemed to be fast, but he was glad it didn't take long to find a job that was compatible with his credentials and was suited for him. His interview was with the man who oversaw HR and was closely associated with the president of the company.

After rising early and working out in the hotel gym, he was ready to make a good impression at his first interview. He drove to the office building and went into Justice Medical. He told the secretary why he was there, and she informed her boss of his arrival. She took him to the human resource office and introduced him to her boss.

"Good afternoon, Mr. Baker. Thanks for seeing me on

such short notice."

Bob Baker, a tall, slender, athletic man in his forties with brown hair and sky-blue eyes greeted Brock with his dazzling smile and strong handshake.

"Nice to meet you, Brock. Thanks for emailing me your résumé and talking with me over the phone yesterday. I'm quite impressed!"

Following the interview, which lasted for an hour and a half, they had discussed every aspect of the job including possibilities of promotions and raises.

Mr. Baker said, "It looks like your move to Nashville could prove to be beneficial for both of us! I've been looking for someone with your credentials, someone with flexibility, motivation, and someone adventurous, willing to take on new job prospects and ready to take on the world."

"Well, if that's what you are looking for, I'm your man!"

"That's superb!" Mr. Baker said as he reached out to shake Brock's hand. "Look over the financial and benefits package and if it meets all your expectations, the job is yours."

He led Brock to the conference room to look over the proposal. After around twenty minutes, he came back to find out Brock's decision. Brock thought the package was more than adequate and told Bob he was satisfied with it.

"Great," Bob said. "Then I will see you next Monday."

"That's perfect, Mr. Baker."

"I'll have them set up your office and it will be overlooking the state capitol."

"Thank you, Mr. Baker, I'm looking forward to working with you."

"Likewise, Brock, and call me Bob."

"Will do, Bob."

Wow! What an interview, and I actually got the job with only one interview. Bob is a really nice guy. The financial and benefit packages were much more than I'd expected for being a new hire to the company. I'm sure I'm going to love living here in Nashville. I think it's the best decision I've ever made!

"He's a shoo-in, Frank. I've never seen someone so eager to please!" Bob chuckled to himself.

"I hope you're right, Bob. We need to get on with our plans. Did you offer him what I suggested?"

"Sure did, Frank. He about leaped out of his chair even though he restrained himself, I'm even going to set him up in the office overlooking the capitol."

"You didn't go overboard did you, Bob?"

"No way, Frank, he's sufficiently mesmerized," Bob smirked.

"Let me know how Monday goes, and you might want to take him to dinner this weekend, just to seal the deal."

"Great idea, Frank. I'll keep you informed of the progress."

Going from a Dental Lab salesperson to a Medical Sales Representative will be somewhat challenging. Even though it's still the medical field, it's a different type of work. I've got a lot to learn, but almost one and a half times my other salary will make it worth all the time and effort I have to put in, Brock thought. *I can't believe I was lucky enough to snag this job on my first interview after only being here a couple of days. I need to upgrade my wardrobe, and get my housing situated. Hopefully, I will be able to do that soon after I start my job. The people I work with should know the best areas in the city to live.* As he was entering his hotel room after some shopping and eating lunch, his phone rang. He dumped his packages on the floor and answered his phone after it rang three times.

"Hey Bob, good to hear from you. Dinner, Saturday?"

"Sure, sounds great, I'll meet you at the steakhouse off

Broadway at 7pm."

Man, they sure do the royal treatment here in Nashville. Think I'm going to be just fine, Brock thought cheerfully.

CHAPTER 4

Carrie had settled in her apartment with phone in hand for the past two hours. She was trying to locate someone who could tell her where Brock was relocating. But she'd hit a brick wall. *Didn't he tell anyone where he was going?* She'd even called his parents in Ohio, and they didn't know anything. They were very concerned. She'd apologized to them and said she didn't mean to worry them she was just trying to get hold of Brock and he wasn't answering his phone and she'd tried reaching him at his apartment and he wasn't there. She was wondering if he'd gone to visit them.

"I'm sure he's fine, and will call when he gets a minute," she said convincingly.

"He's probably just preoccupied with his job and doesn't answer the phone. We had a little spat. He's just mad at me," Carrie told them.

She had called Brock several times, but it always went to voicemail. *Is he never going to talk to me again?* she thought. *I'll just have to keep trying. He'll have to answer eventually. Maybe this time I'll apologize by voicemail. He loved me and wanted to marry me! I should have never gone out with Josh, but the charisma between us was electrifying. Brock was a good dependable man and had a great salary. Surely, I can make him understand if he'd just pick up the phone. I can't let him get away with just leaving like this. After all, who will buy me the house of my dreams, and support my obsession with clothes? Certainly, he told one of his friends where he was moving. Maybe I'll try to reach his closest friends to see if they know.* But after trying a couple of friends, she ran into a dead end.

Brock hung up from talking to his parents, frustrated after discovering that Carrie had called them. *She needs to leave me and my family alone. I want to put the past behind me and want her out of my life. I've got too much to look forward to here in Nashville to be looking behind me and taking care of the messes Carrie makes. Isn't that what the Bible says? Putting the past behind and straining toward what is ahead? I remember the pastor at church preaching on that topic a long time ago. I really need to get my life and faith back on track. I'm looking forward to working in a new environment and meeting new people. Speaking of new people, I'd better get ready to meet Bob at the steakhouse at 7 pm. I'm already excited to explore the medical sales field with him and to meet the rest of the staff.*

"Yes, Frank, I'm on my way there now. I'll discern the situation and see how soon we can get on with our plans. Be patient, it will happen in good time. I know you are anxious to get it off the ground, but we have to give it a little time. I'm here at the steakhouse. Catch you later."

Brock was getting out of the car when Bob pulled in. He walked over to Bob's car so they could walk in together.

"Brock, good to see you again," Bob said while extending his hand. "Getting all settled in?"

"Sure thing, Bob. I'm getting to know Nashville a little bit and falling in love with the place. Seems like a great fit for me."

"That's good to hear," Bob replied. "There's plenty of activity and available places to live around here. This is an active and growing town. Lots of people from all walks of life, music on every corner."

"Yes, I can't wait to find an apartment and get out of the hotel."

"You don't sing or play an instrument do you, Brock."

"Well, now that you mention it, I do play guitar and sing a little."

Amused Bob said, "maybe you'll be the next George Jones singing somewhere here in Nashville."

"I don't know about that," Brock said with a chuckle,

"but I might try out some of the venues around here when I get the time."

"Let me know when you do, maybe I'll come hear you," Bob said with a grin.

They were seated at the table after a fifteen-minute wait, and talked about the city, the best apartments in and around Nashville, the places to go and things to do in the area while eating their steak dinner, which was cooked to perfection. Bob said they'd talk about work later, he just wanted to get to know Brock some.

"Thanks for the invitation to dinner tonight, it's been a real treat. I'm really looking forward to diving in on Monday. Can't wait to learn all there is to know about the medical sales field."

"That's good to hear Brock. I'm looking forward to our new venture with you. The partners were impressed with your résumé as well. You have a good weekend, Brock, and rest up so we can hit the ground running!"

CHAPTER 5

Calling Frank after leaving Brock, Bob said "We've got ourselves a good one, Frank. I think you will be most pleased," Bob said reassuringly. "I'd say after training, we'd be able to get our plans off and running in a couple of months. He is more than willing to do what he can to please. We will have to be very discreet going in, but after he's hooked, he'll be in too deep to get out without consequences."

"I'm trusting you with this one, Bob. Don't let me down," Frank cautioned.

"You worry too much, Frank. I've got it in the bag!"

Frank Callahan, the president of the company, a gruff, greedy, impatient, matter-of-fact person is ready to go forward with their newest venture at Justice Medical. He doesn't want any delays. Bob is always trying to pacify him.

So, Brock is in Nashville! Carrie said enthusiastically to herself while sheepishly grinning. It had taken her a couple of weeks to locate him. He'd finally contacted a friend in Pennsylvania. *What a stroke of luck that I have a childhood friend there.* Sherry Merced and Carrie had been friends since middle school. Sherry and Carrie were cheerleaders then. Sherry was a little shy; had long golden-brown hair, big brown eyes and a smile that broke every guy's heart. She didn't lack friends because of her sweet and friendly personality. She and Carrie were very different, but that's what made their friendship special. Sherry grounded Carrie when she got out of hand with shopping and boys back in the day. Her parents moved to Nashville when her dad got transferred with his job. Sherry was a senior in high school and didn't want to leave. But she found friends quickly and adjusted to her new environment. They'd kept in touch through the years, but actually hadn't spoken in little over a year.

"Sherry, hi! This is Carrie." She thought she should chat for a bit instead of pouncing on Sherry with the intent of her call.

After a few minutes of small talk and catching up, she said, "I just heard that my ex-fiancé is in Nashville. I'd like to make a trip down there. Sherry, I've called several hotels, and they are all booked. I was wondering if I might stay at your place when I come down in a couple of weeks?"

"That would be great to have you come for a visit

Carrie, but I've got friends coming to visit for the week. They've been planning to come for a few months, and they want to see the job prospects in Nashville while they are here. It seems like everyone wants to move to Nashville these days. I'm so sorry to hear it didn't work out for you and Brock. He appeared to be such a nice guy. Maybe you could stay with a friend of mine, Sabrina. She's single and has a nice apartment, if you have to come that weekend. I'll call to see if she's able to offer you a room."

"Sherry that would be fantastic! Tell her I'm willing to compensate her for the room if I can stay there. I really need to talk to Brock. Call me back as soon as you find out something."

Man, what a disappointment that I can't stay with her, Carrie thought. *I have to have a conversation with Brock soon. Maybe if he can hear my side of the story, we can get back together. Nashville wouldn't be such a bad place to live.* That evening, Carrie got a call from Sabrina.

"Sherry told me you needed a place to stay while you're in Nashville. I'd be glad to have you stay with me. What time do you think you'd be getting here? I usually stay out late on Friday evenings, you know, to celebrate the weekend! Tell you what, I'll leave the key under the flowerpot by my door, if I'm not here when you arrive, just make yourself at home."

"Thanks so much Sabrina for your hospitality. I can't

tell you what this means to me. You're so nice to allow me to stay with you."

Wow, That's a relief. Glad to know that I have a place to stay. Brock is going to be so shocked when he sees me. Monday can't get here soon enough.

I'm so excited to begin a new life here in Nashville and the apartment I found has everything I need. I'm sure going to enjoy the pool, hot tub, and fitness center now that I'm settled in my new place, Brock thought while driving to work on Monday. Arriving at the Justice Medical Building, Brock was looking for a parking space, and suddenly he saw one with his name on it. *You've got to be kidding me! They gave me a designated parking place too, and so fast. These guys know how to give you the preferential treatment!* He parked his car and took a deep breath before he got out. *Well, here I come Nashville! Let's get this show on the road.* As he got to his 3rd floor office, Bob met him in the reception area.

"Welcome Brock! Hope you are ready to get your new career up and running."

"I can't wait to get started," Brock said.

"We will begin with the training sessions. You can learn all about our products. With your selling experience, I'm sure it will take no time for you to learn everything. And then once you've trained, I'm sure the promotions will come and all the compensation you deserve," Bob said with a sly chuckle.

"Thanks for the vote of confidence, Bob. It's good to know I have your support, especially in a new town and with a new job."

The day was filled with instructional videos, and a tour of the building. Lunch was catered, and Brock was introduced to all the employees. There was a lot to learn in the medical sales field, but Brock was so excited, he knew he was up to the task. *Wow! Bob said it wouldn't take me long before I got a promotion. He must have a lot of confidence in my abilities already. This job is certainly good for my ego especially after the devastating relationship with Carrie and having to start over in a new place. But I'm really glad that's behind me. I really appreciate the fact that this company is willing to take a chance on me.* With the first two weeks under his belt, he felt like he needed to give himself a special reward. *Think I'll go to The Cowboy Grill that I saw downtown and take my guitar. I heard this place was one of the most popular venues in town. It's local talent night, maybe I can get on stage and give it a try.*

He made his way to his apartment and was thankful he had found one so quickly. With the perks of a gym and pool he would be able to stay fit without a fitness club membership. Changing his clothes, he was glad he had made the decision to buy the boots, he thought with a grin.

Too bad I didn't get the Stetson that I saw. He considered grabbing a bite to eat, but decided The Cowboy Grill would probably have something he could eat. He got his guitar and got directions on his GPS. As he was driving in the heavy traffic around Nashville, he daydreamed about his new job and how he could sell the products for Justice Medical. As he pulled into the parking lot of The Cowboy Grill, he was amazed at how many cars were already there. *It looks like it's a packed house tonight.* Brock took his guitar and signed up to sing. *Looks like it's 10:00 p.m. for me. Can't wait to see what kind of talent they have here.* Brock sat down at the bar, got a drink, something to eat, and settled in.

He talked to a few people that were sitting around him. *Nice people here, down to earth.* He listened to the singers as they gave their all on stage. Some were good; others were a little unpolished. A few had their own unique style and sound, while others just sounded a little more 'karaoke.' *In Nashville, you have to be really talented to get anywhere with your music.* As 10 p.m. rolled around he finally heard, "Brock Morgan you're on." Brock got on stage and began to sing "He Stopped Loving Her Today," a classic country song by George Jones. The room went silent. As he continued to sing, he saw a few tears being wiped away. As he finished, it was still silent. Then one by one, people started to clap and stand. The whole room filled with applause, and as he thanked the crowd he stood to leave. They were asking for another song. The emcee asked Brock if he had another and he began to strum on his guitar; "She Thinks I Still Care," another classic country song. The crowd gave a rousing standing ovation even before the song finished. The emcee came out and told Brock he hoped he'd come back again.

"Folks, we may have a star on our hands!" the emcee said as the crowd cheered.

Brock was amazed at the response he received. As he was leaving, a girl approached him. She introduced herself and told him how impressed she was with him. She said she didn't usually do this kind of thing, but she gave him her name and phone number and told him to call her sometime. She knew he was new in town, and she'd be glad to show him around, no strings attached. He thanked her and put her number in his wallet. *Well, that was nice*, he thought to himself. *She seemed genuinely nice, a good person. She's cute, I may have to call her.* By the time he got home, he was excited but exhausted after a hard week. The weekend ended up being non-eventful after Friday's performance at The Grill. He knew he should find a church to go to on Sunday, but it had been a while since he'd gone. Since he'd been with Carrie, he'd gotten out of the habit of going to church. It hadn't seemed important to her, so he'd just let it go by the wayside. *Guess it's time to get ready for another big week at the Justice Medical Group. Hope this week goes as well as last week.*

CHAPTER 6

Bob and Brock arrived at work at the same time.

"Arriving early, I see," Bob said with a grin, and as he shook hands with Brock he added. "Good to have such an eager employee."

"Well Bob, I'm loving the job and anxious to learn more."

"Good to see the ambition, buddy." Bob chuckled to himself and thought it wouldn't hurt to add a little personal touch to speed up the process. As they entered the building together, Bob said he'd talk to Brock later, he had a meeting to attend. As Bob made his way to his office Frank caught him off guard coming out of his office. Frank Callahan, being the President of the company, had his own ambitions to buy the company someday.

"Bob, can I see you for a minute?" Bob entered Frank's office and took a seat. "Bob how are things going with our new employee?"

"Great Frank, I think he'll be ready in a couple of months if not sooner."

"That's good to hear. I'm getting more anxious to get this off the ground."

"We just have to be patient for the right time, Frank."

"I know, but time is money, Bob."

"I'll keep you informed, Frank. If it's sooner than I expect, I'll give you a heads-up."

As his second week came to a close, Brock was more excited than ever. He'd completed all the training and was ready to go out in the field. He'd be working with a girl he hadn't met yet, but she'd been with the company two and a half years and had a great track record in production and sales. She was being promoted to Director of Sales and would come out of the field. He hoped he did as well as she had. Arriving home, Brock decided to place an order for Chinese food and relax. After checking the stations on TV, watching a movie seemed to be the appropriate thing to do after a vigorous week. Being exhausted, he fell asleep midway through the action-packed movie. A knock on the door awakened Brock from his sleep. He wasn't expecting anyone because he hadn't really met anyone but his coworkers. He opened the door, and there stood the last person he expected to see, Carrie.

"What are you doing here, Carrie?"

As he was shutting the door, she stuck her foot in its way and held out her arm to stop him from closing it, she asked Brock to talk with her.

"I'm sorry, Brock!" and she burst into tears.

He always had a soft spot for teary-eyed girls, so he let her in. As she dabbed a tear, she thanked him for hearing her out. Carrie knew if she turned on the tears, she could get her way. It always worked with Brock. She sat down on the couch, hoping he'd sit beside her. As he sat down in the chair, he stoically told her to go on. She explained what had happened with her and Josh and apologized profusely for her mistake.

"I realize you are sorry, Carrie, but I've moved on, and I don't have any room for you in my life now."

"But Josh, I mean Brock, you don't mean that!"

Brock jumped up and opened the door and motioned for her to leave, "Get out, Carrie!"

Carrie picked up her purse, apologizing and crying as she tried to persuade Brock to give her another chance. As she walked out the door, he slammed the door behind her.

"And don't come back!" Brock yelled.

Darn it! I was doing so well, till I called Brock by Josh's name, Carrie said to herself. *I could just kick myself.* As she left, she decided she didn't want to waste the trip to Nashville so she tried to figure out what she would do now that her relationship with Brock was finally over in her mind. *Guess I'll have to call Josh and apologize to him for breaking it off with him. I'll tell him I really miss him, and I've changed my mind. We can still see each other. Since I'll be here in Nashville for a few days, I might as well make the most of it. I'll invite him to join me here.* She called Josh and because he'd had a hectic week and needed a change of scenery, he told Carrie he'd be there if he could get a flight. Carrie was happy to hear that because she didn't want this trip to be in vain. *Sabrina has a large apartment, and he can stay there.*

After the encounter with Carrie, Brock decided to work out in the gym. She had stirred up some negative emotions he thought he'd gotten over. He was irritated and angry at her for coming here. Reflecting on that, he remembered talking with the girl he'd met at The Grill last weekend. She seemed to be a decent person, unlike Carrie. When he got back to his apartment, he called her. Apologizing for the late call, he asked her if she'd like to get together. She said she would be happy to show him around and told him she'd meet him at the local coffee shop in the morning around 10 a.m. to get some coffee and head out. The next morning as he entered the coffee shop looking for her, she approached him. Janice was a cute bubbly 5'2" girl with reddish hair and lighter highlights. He could have easily overlooked her because of her stature. But she had a gentle yet commanding presence about her and her eyes were as green as jade, yet had a softness about them. They properly introduced themselves at The Coffee House.

"Hi Brock, I'm Janice Tyler. So glad you called. I hope I wasn't too forward giving you my number, but you seemed like such a nice guy, and you were unfamiliar with the area. I thought you might need some assistance getting around and having someone local showing you is the best way to do it. I'm usually not that aggressive," she said blushing.

"That's okay, Janice, I'm glad you did. I needed someone who's lived here awhile to show me the ropes."

"Let's start by seeing some of the basic stores, and then we'll go by a few restaurants, after that I'll show you some of the night life. How did you learn to play and sing? You were awesome!"

"I was taught to play the guitar and a little piano by my grandfather. He was a great guy and I sure do miss him. He sang and played guitar in a local country band back in Ohio for around thirty-five years. I'm an old soul and love classic country songs like my grandfather sang. I also got some experience singing in a few of the plays in high school, nothing professional and got over my stage fright," he said jokingly.

After a few hours together, they decided to meet for dinner at a local Italian restaurant. They parted ways around midafternoon. After resting a little, Brock cleaned up and picked Janice up around 7 p.m. for dinner. They enjoyed the evening laughing and talking. It seemed they'd always known each other. Reminiscing on the day and evening with Janice, Brock knew he wanted to get to know her more.

CHAPTER 7

What a weekend, Carrie thought. *I was surprised when Josh agreed to fly to Nashville. I'm glad he was able to stay at Sabrina's. She has plenty of room in her apartment. He's such a great guy and the charisma we have is still there. Maybe it was a good thing it didn't work out for me and Brock,* she thought. *Nashville is a wonderful place, but it's not a place I'd like to live. Living in a city like New York or somewhere exciting is more my style, more refined and so much to do. It may be more expensive to live there, but I'm sure it would be worth it. Living in Pennsylvania is nice, but I need a change. Yes, someplace like New York would let me expand my horizons. Maybe Josh and I can travel there to see if there's a place we'd like to live and maybe we could look for jobs there, too. I'm sure we are going to get married at some point in our relationship. We seem like such a good match. Josh has a good corporate job and a decent salary. Maybe not as much as Brock, but it can work for us.*

"Ready to start a new week, Brock?" Bob said slyly.

"I'm up for it and I can't wait to get out in the field."

"Brock, I'd like you to meet Sabrina Carpenter. She'll be your trainer in the field. She's made a name for herself here at Justice Medical. She's one of the best in the business as far as we're concerned."

Brock was mesmerized by her stunning professional appearance. Her golden-brown hair and piercing brown eyes, not to mention her shapely 5'9" frame would make any guy take a second look.

"Glad to meet you, Sabrina. I hope I can live up to your standard."

"Sorry I haven't met you until now. I was on vacation when you arrived and have also been busy with guests from out-of-town. But from what I've heard, Brock, your future sounds very promising here," Sabrina stated. "Well, I guess we should get started. I'll meet you in the lobby in twenty minutes after I get my things."

"Sounds good, Sabrina."

"You both enjoy your day out in the field," Bob said.

"We will," Brock responded.

The first day in the field meeting clients went well. Sabrina took Brock to meet ten of her clients. If they could meet that many each day, in a couple more weeks he would know all the clients. Brock impressed the people he met. He had a charismatic personality that drew people to him. Even though they would miss Sabrina, they knew Brock was a good fit for the job and welcomed him with enthusiasm. They stayed together in the field for six weeks.

"Well Brock, I think it's time to turn you loose on Nashville!" Sabrina said with a laugh. "I know you will do great. Just remember you sell products people need. You just make sure they know they need them!"

They laughed and talked about how much they enjoyed working together. Sabrina was a very professional person. She was beautiful with her long, golden-brown hair. Her large brown eyes had a glint in them that was endearing. As they departed ways, after they got back to the office, Sabrina went to talk to Bob. They discussed how the next few weeks would be handled and made out a business plan for the next six months.

"Now that it's been more than two months, Bob, what's Brock's status?"

"Frank, I can't believe he fell into our lap," Bob chuckled. "He's a tremendous asset. I'm going to begin the process next week. We'll be swimming in money by springtime. Sabrina says she's never seen a more gullible man. He believes everything he's told," Bob said as their laughter roared and they made further plans.

As they continued to talk, they decided to discuss how

to promote *Milagro*. They had already talked over different ideas for moving forward with the product.

"Frank, I think promoting the medical weight loss diet is the way to go. I know we've talked of other ways, but it seems to me that this sounds like the most convincing way. We can offer a diet and exercise plan along with a daily pill regimen, and by the time they take a few pills, and the weight starts falling off, they'll be hooked. I think we can start by promoting it through the elite weight loss spas. Then we can go to the fitness clubs. We'll tell Brock it's a way to expand our business, and with his capable leadership, we can promote him as the business broadens."

After they defined the strategy, Bob agreed to meet with Brock on Monday morning to unveil the plan.

CHAPTER 8

Brock was a little surprised that the company was bringing out a new product just as he was coming on board. But he was assured that everything would be fine. They decided that Sabrina would work with some of the sales staff to determine who would be the best person to take over Brock's job with the company, and that Brock would solely take on the new product so he wouldn't be overwhelmed. Sabrina would tell the clients that Brock was such an asset to the company that he was the ideal person to promote and sell the new product the company was developing. Someone else in the sales field would take over the job they'd planned for Brock and Sabrina would introduce them to the clients. That was agreeable to Brock. So, he began learning all he could about the new products they were creating and how to present them. He looked up some elite spas and became familiar with the staff. After a couple of weeks, he started telling the spa managers about the product he had and how well it would work for their clients. They were impressed by what they heard and decided to order several cases of the product because they had a lot of clients that would be interested. After his relationship with them was established, he went on to the fitness clubs and sold to them as well. With the new plan in progress, Brock was at the top of his game. He never dreamed that a weight loss plan could be in such high demand and that selling it would be so easy. *I guess these guys know their business. The weight loss system is selling like hot cakes! People want easy and fast when it comes to losing weight. This appears to be quite the combination.* After three months of selling, the fitness clubs saw tremendous progress in their clients' weight loss, and the clients were feeling better than they'd ever felt. They started returning for more of the product not wanting to be without it.

"Hi Brock, it's been a while," Janice replied.

"I know, Janice. I've meant to call, but I've been working nonstop with the new expansion at Justice. I've really missed seeing you. You want to go to The Grill Friday night?"

"Sure, you think you have time for it?"

"I'm going to make the time, Janice. All work and no play... you know?"

"Well, I'm glad to hear you are doing so well in your job, but I've really missed the times we spent together."

"Hey, do you sing, Janice? Maybe we could be the next George Jones and Tammy Wynette," he said with a laugh.

"I can sing a little, but I've never done any performing. Brock, you'll do just fine by yourself. It's nice talking and laughing with you again, Brock. I'll see you Friday night."

"Thanks for the vote of confidence, Sabrina. It all seems to be going smoothly. I never dreamed a weight loss system could be in such a high demand."

"Well, Brock, everyone wants to look their best especially if it's easy. That's why the *Milagro* Weight Loss System is so successful. *Milagro* means 'miracle' in Spanish," Sabrina told Brock. "With healthy meals planned out for a month, and a pill a day, you can't get any easier than that! I wish I'd come up with the idea, I'd be a rich girl by now! Keep up the good work! Brock, I hear a promotion could be just around the corner for you!"

"Thanks for all your help, Sabrina."

"Hey Brock, you know we should go out Friday night. There's a great new restaurant I'm dying to try. Why don't I pick you up at 7 pm. Got to run, see you Friday."

Wow, I can't believe Sabrina asked me out. I never dreamed she'd even consider a date with me. How in the world did I manage to hit the jackpot moving to Nashville?

While headed home with his mind in the clouds, he suddenly remembered his date with Janice for Friday night. Guess I'd better call her and reschedule.

"Hey Janice, something's come up on Friday, and I'm going to have to postpone our date. No, nothing's wrong... it's just work related...sorry. Why don't we make plans for the following Friday, and I promise I won't cancel on you again. Okay. talk with you soon."

She's such an understanding person, I hate to cancel on her, but duty calls!

"Hey Brock, you about to wrap it up for the day? I'm starving and can't wait to try out that new Italian Restaurant."

"Be with you in just a couple of minutes, Sabrina. As soon as I take care of this last entry."

Sabrina stepped outside of Brock's office and made a call to Bob to give him an update. As she hung up, Brock came out and locked his door.

"I'm ready now. Are we driving separate cars?"

"Sure, that way we won't have to come back to pick up a car."

"You're the boss," Brock said.

Sabrina grinned with a beguiling smile, "Let's go. I'm starved."

They settled in at the restaurant, ordered a glass of wine, and looked at the menu. After ordering the special on the menu for the evening, the conversation was geared around work.

"I've been looking forward to our evening out, Sabrina."

"So have I, Brock. You're a really energetic and driven guy, and it appears your work is very gratifying for you."

"It is, Sabrina. I've never been as enthusiastic about a job."

"It doesn't seem as if they are taking advantage of you," she said. "There are always rewards for your hard work. That would be an incentive for anyone. They have been good to me as well, Brock. I'm hoping you'll be around a long time. I'm looking forward to getting to know you on a more personal basis," Sabrina said with a flirting smile.

Brock nearly choked on his drink. *Does she really want us to be more than colleagues,* Brock thought with anticipation. Then he remembered Carrie, and that stifled his excitement. They continued to talk and eat dinner. As Brock looked at his watch, he couldn't believe how fast the time had flown by.

"I can't believe it's as late as it is. We've been here nearly three hours, Sabrina."

"Well, you know what they say, time flies when you're having fun. Let's go out again tomorrow night."

"Really? Are you sure?"

"Of course, I'm sure Brock or I wouldn't have mentioned it. Why don't you come to my place for a pizza and a movie."

"That's sounds relaxing, what time?"

"Seven o'clock okay with you?"

"I'll be there. Normally, I'd take my date home, but since we came from work, guess I'll see you to your car."

As she got into her car Brock said, "Be careful going home, Sabrina."

"Sure thing, Brock. See you tomorrow evening."

I think I've outclassed myself this time, he thought as he watched her pull away from the parking lot in her brand-new shiny black Mercedes. *She's such an attractive, competent, and empathetic person. I think I could fall hard if I let myself. But I'm not getting involved with someone I work with; however, we can be friends,* Brock thought with a smile while getting into his own car.

After Sabrina got in her car, she gave Bob a quick text about the evening. Bob called Frank following Sabrina's text.

"It's going just as we planned Frank. He's getting in a little deeper. He'll be hooked and won't be able to get out soon."

CHAPTER 9

"Sherry? Hi, it's Carrie."

"Hi Carrie, good to hear from you. Coming back to Nashville?"

"I've been thinking about it."

"Did you ever hear from Brock?"

"No, I think I officially ruined my chances with him while I was there. I was trying to get hold of Sabrina, but her phone goes to voicemail. I think I left a dress there. I can't seem to find it. Do you talk to her much?"

"No, she's been working a lot. She seems to be involved in a new product launch with her company. I guess it keeps her busy. She recently got a promotion and with training the new guy and the product launch she's hardly ever home. You still seeing Josh? He seemed like a great guy and the attraction between you two was evident," Sherry said with a laugh.

"I think he's going to ask me to marry him soon. We've been very happy together."

Their conversation lasted about half an hour, catching up on each other's lives.

"It's been great talking to you Sherry. When you talk to Sabrina would you mind asking her about my dress and telling her hello for me and thanks again for the hospitality?"

"Sabrina, thanks for the invitation. You have a beautiful condo and look at the view of the river!"

"Thanks, Brock. Come on in and make yourself at home. The pizza is on its way along with a couple of salads. Let's have a glass of wine while we wait."

They talked a little about work and living in Nashville, but Brock wanted to know more about her.

"Tell me about your family and where you grew up, Sabrina."

"I grew up in California. After I graduated high school, I went to college there, and got a degree in marketing. Later I decided to move to Nashville because I'd heard it was a great place to live and jobs were plentiful. It was tough leaving my friends, but I made some good friends here, and kept a relationship with a few friends from California. But people move on to other things. Hold that thought. Got a text from the pizza guy. The pizza is here."

"Thanks Sam, here's your tip."

"Wow, thanks Sabrina. You tip the most of any of my customers."

"Maybe you can save up for new wheels, Sam."

"That's a great idea, I could use a new car, I'm really racking up the miles on this one."

"Have a great evening Sam."

"Thanks Sabrina, you, too."

"He's such a nice guy, he'd do just about anything for anyone. Now let's eat before the pizza gets cold. Where were we? Oh yeah, tell me about your family, Brock."

"I grew up in Ohio, my parents are still living there. I went to college there as well, studying business management. I met a guy in one of my classes who was from Pennsylvania. We became close friends. He moved back to Pennsylvania after college. In pursuit of a job, I decided to move there. I located the job with Dental Lab Sales and was there for ten years until I moved to Nashville. I needed a new start. I have a brother, Cal, who lives in Connecticut. He's three years older than me. He's the CEO of a construction company there. Do you have any siblings, Sabrina?"

"No, I'm an only child. I always wished I'd had a sister

but wishful thinking, I guess."

They continued to talk about their lives as they ate dinner, although Sabrina tried to get Brock to talk more about himself so she could keep her life more private, not wanting to reveal too much. When he asked about her life again, she gave a couple of trivial answers.

"Let's get this cleaned up, then we can watch the movie. I've got this great movie I'm dying to see. You do like romantic movies don't you, Brock?"

"Umm, sure," Brock said with hesitation.

"Oh, I just knew you would," Sabrina said with excitement.

She opened another bottle of wine before they hunkered down for the evening to watch the movie. Sabrina lit the fireplace and moved to sit closer to Brock.

"Is it okay if I sit here?" Sabrina said innocently.

"Sure," Brock said hesitantly.

He'd been mesmerized by Sabrina since he met her. This evening felt surreal. As the movie progressed Sabrina leaned her head on Brock's shoulder, subsequently he put his arm around her. As the movie drew to an end, Sabrina leaned over and kissed him. Brock was enticed even more. He needed to get out of her apartment before things got out of hand.

"Well, um, Sabrina, this has been a great evening, but it's getting late, and I think I should be going."

"Oh, Brock, do you have to?" she said as she put her arms around him.

"Yes, I'm sure I do," he chuckled as he nudged her gently away.

"Oh well, I'll see you tomorrow afternoon for lunch then. Maybe we could take a stroll through the park? I love being with you and talking to you."

"Okay, Sabrina that sounds fine, I'll see you around noon."

"Great, I can't wait!"

As Brock drove home, somewhat in a daze, he reminisced about their evening. *How in the world could all of this be happening to me? A dream job, and now a wonderful woman interested in me.* As his thoughts moved forward to someday becoming the CEO of Justice Medical, he started thinking about his date for Saturday with Sabrina and then remembered that he'd promised to go out with Janice next weekend. He'd already messed up a couple of times and had to cancel. He'd have to tell her he's met someone at work. She was too nice of a girl to let her think there might be something between them. Although he did like her a lot and enjoyed being with her. Their relationship was comfortable, and they had a lot in common. She was funny and they got along great. Maybe he'd go out with her sometime just as friends. Maybe lunch at the deli they liked. As Brock got closer to home, he turned up the radio to hear the latest news.

"WHOW reporting a death of a prominent local celebrity. More details to follow as we have them."

Wow I wonder who that was? I'll have to listen to the late news when I get home to see if there are any more details. He turned down the radio and pulled into his garage. His phone started to ring.

"Brock Morgan here."

"Hey Brock, I was thinking, instead of lunch why don't we do dinner tomorrow night. I'll cook."

"That's sounds great, Sabrina, I'll see you about 7 p.m. then."

Saturday was a relaxing day for Brock. Anticipating baseball season, he turned on the sports network to watch a few reruns of his favorite team. The phone rang and Brock answered only to find Josh on the other end questioning him about Carrie. *Man, that girl is like a bad penny, her name keeps coming up.*

"Josh, I really can't tell you anything further, and frankly, I'm surprised you called me. Can't say I blame you if you want to break off the relationship with her, though."

They talked a few more minutes and Brock gave him what advice he could. He sort of felt sorry for Josh. He knew what it was like to have a relationship with Carrie. Josh said he would let him know what happened after he talked with Carrie. Brock wished him the best. After all, he did him a favor when he went out with her. Even though it caused him some hurt initially, it was the best thing that could have happened to him. He wouldn't have moved to Nashville, and he loved it here. *Everything always works out for a reason.*

CHAPTER 10

With time slipping away, Brock decided to take a shower before going to Sabrina's for dinner. After he got out of the shower, he saw that Janice had called. *I really need to talk with her. I'll text her that I'm busy and I'll call her later.* After arriving at Sabrina's, they ate dinner and talked for hours. Sabrina told Brock that she was going to suggest that he be promoted to manager of the sales department on Monday. She thought that he was ready for it. He'd had such success with sales in the past six months with over $1 million in sales already.

"We know you are the best at sales, and we want you to start training other recruits. You are such an asset to the company, Brock. And you are pretty special to me."

Brock didn't know what to say. He got so excited that he picked Sabrina up and swirled her around and kissed her. It kind of surprised Brock that he reacted that way, but Sabrina had become special to him as well.

"Well, I'd better leave on that note," Brock said with a

grin. Sabrina knew she had him now.

"Well let's just have one more kiss before you leave," Sabrina said with an appealing smile. After they kissed again, he knew they'd become a lot more than just friends and coworkers. They had a very personal connection.

When Monday morning came, Brock entered the third-floor lobby greeted by Bob.

"Why don't you come into my office Brock."

As they entered the office Brock took a seat. After a few minutes of chit chat, Bob offered him the manager of sales position, which happened to be a new position created especially for him.

"As we ventured out into this new field with *Milagro*, Brock, you took the lead in exploring new areas of sales and we are grateful for all you've contributed. Of course, a raise is in order, a small one of $40,000 annually."

Brock nearly fell out of his chair but kept his composure.

"There's money to be made in the field, and as we prosper you will too, Brock. You've worked hard and we want you to know that we notice your dedication to the company."

As Brock stood to leave, they shook hands. Brock went to his office. Shocked, to say the least, he called Sabrina and told her of his promotion. He thanked her for whatever input she had. *What a whirlwind this job has been. I'm thankful that Justice Medical is such a wonderful company and that I found them after I arrived here.*

Another six months passed, and as he kept getting more involved with the company, his relationship with Sabrina grew deeper. He'd broken off the relationship with Janice and told her he just wanted to be friends. Dropping by from time to time to see her, she saw a drastic change in his behavior. She didn't like what she saw, and tried to tell Brock what she was seeing in him. He didn't listen, of course, and told Janice she was just being too conservative. "Don't be a joy sucker, Janice," he'd say. He enjoyed his new lifestyle and friends. He'd been very generous with her, buying her a new car because her old one kept breaking down. He wanted to take care of his family and friends. He was prosperous and wanted to share his new good fortune.

"Frank, are you satisfied with the way things are going?" asked Bob.

"They are fantastic. Sorry I doubted you, Bob."

"What does Henry have to say?" asked Bob.

"He's pleased that the company is doing so well," Frank replied.

"Does he have any idea why," Bob asked.

"No, he thinks it's just the medical field picking up.

He knows about the new *Milagro* weight loss system but doesn't know anything else. He doesn't need to know," Frank said with a chuckle. "Henry will be retiring soon. I'll step into his position as CEO when I buy him out, or maybe he'll leave it to me in his will since he doesn't have any relatives," Frank said jokingly.

With the way things are going, I think that might be sooner than even I expected, Frank thought to himself. Bob laughed as he left the office shaking his head at Frank, *I hope for Frank's sake he's able to buy Henry out when the time comes.*

Frank turned on the radio in his office just in time to hear a reporter say, "This is WHOW reporting the death of a prominent local businessman who died suddenly this afternoon. More details to follow later on the evening news."

"Everyone at the spas and fitness clubs seems to think the *Milagro* weight loss system is the best thing they have ever tried," Brock told Bob. "People are getting great results with it. It's almost like it's heaven-sent. It's really cool that the diet plan allows people to plan their meals ahead of time as well."

"Yes, Brock, it is quite the phenomenon. Your marketing ideas are what's accelerating it as well. You've done a great job with it. I don't know of anyone else who could have done a better job."

"What ingredients are in the pills, Bob?"

"Oh, our lab did a lot of work on the ingredients with patents pending."

"I've never seen the lab, Bob, I'd like to visit it sometime."

"Sure thing, we'll go there one day when we have some time. They stay pretty busy," Bob replied. *That's not likely. You just go on selling and managing the sales department. We'll take care of the lab,* he thought.

As months passed, Brock continued his relationship with Sabrina. Sales continued to soar with new venues for *Milagro* and the sales team continued to increase. Brock set up a system to order *Milagro* online for the convenience of his customers. After that, the online ordering that was developed boosted sales substantially. Brock began wondering why there hadn't been any acknowledgements of his progress lately. Recognition had come so frequently in the beginning of his time there. He approached Bob and asked if they were still pleased with how sales for the weight loss system were progressing.

"Brock, we were just talking about that and what a marvelous job you continue to do. As we are contemplating a new title for you, Brock, we know there is no one else with the talent for developing new recruits the way you have. We are going to give you a bonus in the meantime of $15,000 until we can work out your advancement."

"Wow, thanks Bob, I really appreciate your generosity," Brock said. "That's quite a bonus."

He really wasn't expecting that, but he had brought millions into the company since launching *Milagro*. As Brock left the company for the day, he phoned Janice to tell her his news.

"That's great," she said. "You are definitely making a name for yourself over there. I'm proud of you. Thanks for sharing your good news with me."

"You're my best friend, Janice. Why wouldn't I?"

"I know we are best friends, and that's why I wish you'd consider going back to The Cowboy Grill again. You've got such a great talent I would love to see you use it more."

"Maybe one day I'll go back there. I just don't have a lot of time right now, but I appreciate your encouragement in the vocal department. It really is a lot of fun going there. Well, have to go now. I'll talk with you later, Janice."

"Okay, Brock." And as Janice hung up the phone, she whispered a prayer for him. *Oh God, please help Brock to find you again. Help him to realize he's not using the great voice for singing that you've gifted him with and help him realize how much time he's spending at his job. Help him to have a more balanced life.*

"Frank, I called Henry today," Bob said. "He said he's been under the weather here lately. Has a bug that he can't shake."

"Yes, I know I talked with him recently. I'm not sure what's going on, but I plan on going over there tonight to see him. I'll let you know how he's doing."

He won't be getting better any time soon if I can help it, Frank thought with a hearty laugh as he hung up the phone. *Henry's time is limited. It's time for me to take over the company. I'll be swimming in money when that happens,* he thought greedily. He finished up at work and headed over to Henry's house. As he pulled into Henry's driveway, Frank wondered why Henry never moved into a larger home. *This little dump of a house couldn't be worth more than a quarter of a million dollars. I plan to get a large estate when I take over. Someone with the success of a company like Justice Medical should live in style. Speaking of living in style, I think I'll get a Ferrari. Had my eye on one of those for years now.*

"Hello, Henry how are you tonight?"

"I'm not doing so well, Frank. I've been a little dizzy and not much energy lately. I can't seem to snap out of it. Guess I should make an appointment to see Dr. Radford."

"I'm sure you'll be fine in a few days; sometimes these things take a little longer when you're older. Are you staying hydrated, Henry? Maybe you're dehydrated. That can make you feel tired. Anything I can get for you? A glass of water or tea?"

"Yes, that would be nice, Frank."

"I can't really find anything here, so I'll go pick something up for you. I'll be right back."

He went to the nearest fast-food place to pick up something and brought it back to the house.

"Here you go, Henry. I got two bottles of water, a large tea, a couple of sandwiches and some soup. Maybe you can eat a little now and have some for later since I know you don't feel like cooking. Hope you feel better soon. Can I get you anything else?"

"No, Frank, that's good. Thanks for thinking of me and trying to take care of me."

"That's the least I can do. You just get better. I'll check in on you tomorrow, too."

As Frank was leaving, he noticed some legal papers on the foyer table. He picked them up to peruse them. It was a will with instructions about Henry's personal belongings, but nothing about his business. *I wonder who the beneficiary is on the business. Certainly, he has some document somewhere with the information in it. I'll have to see what I can find out. I'm really surprised he's never mentioned that in all these years working together. Of course, I'll have to make it a priority now,* Frank chuckled to himself.

CHAPTER 11

Early the next day Bob stopped by to see Henry. Knocking on the door several times, he looked in the window and everything seemed to be in order and quiet. He decided to look around back to see if a door might be unlocked. Looking through the kitchen door, he was startled to see Henry lying on the floor, apparently unconscious. Bob called 911, checked the door to see if it was unlocked and looked around for a key but couldn't find one. He broke the glass and unlocked the kitchen door. Henry's breathing was shallow. After a few minutes, the emergency team arrived. They administered the appropriate treatment along with oxygen to Henry and took him to the hospital. Bob called Frank to report what had happened on his way to the hospital. Frank seemed to be alarmed, almost mad, when Bob told him of the incident, which seemed rather strange to Bob.

"You okay, Frank? You seemed to be taking this rather hard."

"Well, I'm just concerned and shocked after I saw Henry yesterday. He didn't seem to be that bad. I was planning to go over there today. What made you stop by? I mean I'm glad you did," Frank said trying to cover his tracks.

Sometimes Bob needs to keep his nose out of other people's business, Frank thought.

"I just hadn't heard from Henry or seen him in a while," Bob said, "and wanted to check on him. He is getting up in age. Hey, I'm here at the hospital now, Frank. I'll call you when I find out something."

"That's okay. I'm on my way there now."

I've got to hear first-hand what the doctors say so I know how to proceed, he thought anxiously. Bob stopped by the emergency room reception desk to find out what room Henry was in. While waiting, Frank walked up to Bob. They found out Henry's room number and walked to his room together. Henry was asleep when they arrived, but woke up a few minutes after, and was glad to see them. They talked for a while. Finally, the doctor came in and told Henry he was going to be fine, just a little dehydrated and weak from the flu. He'd be dismissed tomorrow after he got plenty of fluids in his system. Frank breathed a sigh of relief. Bob told Henry he'd be by to pick him up tomorrow after he was released. Henry thanked Bob and said he was grateful for his help. Bob and Frank left the hospital.

"Frank, are you okay?" Bob asked.

"Yes, I guess I was more shook up over Henry than I realized."

"Well, Frank, he's going to be fine."

Yes, I was afraid of that, Frank thought.

"Guess I'll see you tomorrow, Bob. I've got some things to take care of this afternoon, so I won't be at the office."

"Okay, then I'll catch up with you tomorrow after I pick up Henry."

I've got to get over to Henry's house now to see if I can find his will. I need to know who the beneficiary is of the business. That could make a big difference in how I proceed. I'll have to hurry to see what I can find. I won't be able to turn any lights on or someone will know somebody is in the house. If he has one part of the will here, he must have all of it. I'll search the office first.

How can anyone have such a mess and so many files? After half an hour searching the office to no avail, Frank headed to the kitchen. He found a letter from Henry's lawyer and some other paperwork in the kitchen, but no will. *How can any one person be so unorganized!* After searching the bedroom and the rest of the house, Frank decided to leave. *Maybe I can talk to Henry when he gets home and urge him to get his affairs in order. Then, maybe he will tell me what he has planned.*

Carrie and Josh continued their relationship for a couple of months after he talked to Brock. He was having a difficult time deciding how to break it off with her. Even though Carrie seemed to be in love with him, or as much in love as she could be, given her narcissistic tendencies, Josh knew he couldn't go on with their relationship any further. Finally, he gathered up the courage and decided to call Carrie.

"Carrie, I'd like to come over if that's alright."

"Sure Josh, you know you can come anytime."

"Okay, I'll see you in about an hour."

As they hung up, Carrie thought, *Oh my gosh, he's going to ask me to marry him! I bet he's getting the ring before he comes over. I'm so excited. I'm going to have to call Sherry,* she thought excitedly. As the phone rang several times, she thought Sherry wasn't home. Finally, she answered.

"Sherry, it's Carrie."

"Sorry, Carrie, I was doing laundry and didn't hear it ring. What's up?"

"Josh is going to come over, and I think he's going to propose to me after all this time!"

"I'm so thrilled for you Carrie. You guys have been seeing each other for a while. Are you sure he's 'the one'?"

"Of course, he's the one! We get along so well. We agree on practically everything. Brock and I fought all the time. Aren't you happy for me, Sherry?"

"Of course I am, Carrie, if you're sure."

"I can't wait till he gets here. I think I have just enough time to freshen my makeup and change clothes before he gets here. I'll call you when he leaves."

"Sure thing. I'll be waiting to hear."

They hung up and Carrie freshened up and made sure everything was perfect while waiting on Josh. As she turned on some romantic music, Carrie even practiced how she'd say 'yes!' Josh also rehearsed what he was going to say; he wanted to be as gentle as he could be. He hated to tell Carrie he was breaking up with her, but he just couldn't make her see how selfish she was. He had mostly given in to her, so she'd stop whining when she didn't get her way. That's not a relationship. He wanted more than what she was capable of giving.

Well, here goes nothing, he said to himself as he got into his car. He stopped to get gas, then headed to her house. He prayed that God would give him the words he needed to be kind and gracious. After arriving at her house, he prayed as he got out of the car that God would give him the guidance to say what he needed to say and nothing more. He knocked, and Carrie immediately opened the door with a big smile on her face.

"Josh, I'm so glad you're here, come on in."

"Thanks, Carrie."

"Have a seat. Can I get you something to drink?"

"Sure, water would be fine, thanks."

They talked briefly about trivial things then Josh told her he had something he needed to tell her. Carrie sat on the edge of her chair and told him to go on, with a big smile on her face. Josh started by saying he knew they had dated a long time and there had been some good times.

She blurted out, "Yes! Yes, I'll marry you!"

She got up and threw her arms around him. He was stunned and took her arms and gently pushed her back.

"Carrie, please listen. I'm not finished. I know we've been dating a while, but I feel like we're not suited for each other and that you're not the one for me. I think we should end the relationship."

Carrie was almost speechless.

"But Josh, I thought we were getting along so well, we hardly ever disagree," and she started crying. "Josh, I thought you were going to ask me to marry you! I can't believe you are doing this to me!"

As her voice began to rise, she started to get angry. *This isn't going to end well,* Josh anticipated.

"Carrie, I'm sorry but the reason we've been 'getting along' is because I've been giving in to you. You whine when you don't get your way, and it hasn't been easy to take. A relationship should be about two people not just one."

"How dare you accuse me of whining when I don't get my way! I'm a very giving person!"

"Oh, Carrie, you need a reality check. You are one of the most selfish people I know. I'm sorry it had to end this way, but I have to go before this gets worse."

He opened the door to leave, and as he did, she picked up his glass of water and threw it at him. She missed and he turned to look at her with a disgusted look on his face. Then he slammed the door.

"How dare he treat me like this! He'll be sorry one day!"

Man, I'm glad that's over, Josh thought. *What a weight off my shoulders. I don't know how I stayed with her as long as I did.*

"I guess we better get things back on track now that the scare with Henry is over."

"Yes, that was a little unnerving, Bob."

"Brock seems to be getting a little curious about the lab. I hope it's just a passing thought with him."

"You make sure he doesn't go anywhere near that lab, Bob," Frank replied nervously.

"Oh, I will, Frank. Don't you worry about a thing. I've handled everything pretty well thus far."

"Yes, you have, but one look at what is going on down there, and well, let's just say, our project might come to a crashing halt."

"I know, so trust me to make sure nothing happens."

"Alright, just stay on your guard, Bob."

CHAPTER 12

As Sabrina entered Brock's office, she sneaked up behind him while he was hard at work making sure his statistics were correct on the sale of *Milagro*.

"Hi Brock, you up for a weekend getaway? I thought we could fly to the Bahamas," she said as she waved the tickets in the air.

"What! You're kidding, right?"

"Do I look like I'm kidding with these tickets in my hands? We'll get off at 1:00 p.m. on Friday and drive straight to the airport. Our flight leaves at 3:17 p.m. so make sure you pack your bag before you leave home on Friday. It's a four-hour flight, so we'll get there just before sunset. Just imagine walking on that white sand. I can't wait!"

I can't believe Sabrina did that. I'm not sure I'm totally ready for this, Brock thought with hesitation. *After the relationship with Carrie, I'm not sure I want to go any deeper than we already are. She certainly moves fast. It would be nice to get away, though. To relax and not think about work. Well maybe it won't hurt to go just this once.*

Work was hectic, and Friday couldn't come soon enough. Brock packed his bag before leaving for the office Friday morning. He called Janice and told her he would be away for the weekend but didn't tell her he was going to be with Sabrina. He just said he needed a little R & R. She seemed glad he was getting away. He needed to relax. She said a prayer, once again, as she hung up, that Brock would find his way back to God. She prayed daily for him. One day she would tell him how she felt and how much she prayed for him.

As the plane landed, Sabrina was excited, and Brock was relieved to be away from work to relax. They went to their hotel to check in. Brock was once again overwhelmed. The extravagance of the hotel was over the top. She had gotten a three-bedroom luxury suite for them.

"Sabrina, you really went all out for this weekend."

"Anything for you Brock. Let's get ready to go to the beach to see the sunset. I'll call room service for a picnic basket and a bottle of wine. Then we'll head out to the private cabana."

After they got their basket, they found a perfect spot on the beach to watch the sunset. They settled in, enjoying the beach and the excellent food and wine while relaxing.

"This is just gorgeous. I'm so glad we came, Brock. What a weekend this is going to be!"

Brock was torn between having fun and anxiety. Something just didn't feel right, but he decided since Sabrina had gone to all the trouble to set up the weekend, he should just go along with it this time. After all, he did like her, but things just seemed to be accelerating too quickly.

The next day was full of activity. Starting the day with coffee and breakfast at the infinity pool, they spent the afternoon snorkeling and parasailing. That evening they walked on the beach and had dinner at the hotel's restaurant on their outdoor patio watching the sun set. As they were enjoying their fresh Caribbean conch with lime, rice, and a basket of johnnycakes, Brock was looking at Sabrina and wondering what she was thinking about their relationship.

"This has certainly been a delightful weekend, Sabrina. However, I do want you to know that as much as I like you and enjoy being with you, I'm not sure I'm ready for another serious relationship. My last one didn't end well."

"Sabrina almost choked on her food but composed herself.

"Oh Brock, that's all right. I just enjoy being with you, and thought we needed a break from work. We've both been working so hard, and it's been so hectic."

"I know, and I really appreciate all the effort you put

into this weekend. It's really been quite captivating."

Sabrina smiled at Brock. *Well, this isn't going quite as planned,* she thought while hoping for more. She guessed she'd have to figure out another way to make him fall harder for her. She just knew this would do it. They were seeing a lot of each other. *I guess I thought him more gullible than he is. There's plenty more I can do and will do to make him fall for me. But it's imperative that it be soon.*

"Let's get another bottle of wine and just enjoy our time here. It's so beautiful," she said.

As they watched the waves crashing on the beach and the sun setting, it certainly was paradise. *I just can't imagine anyone not falling in love in this setting,* she thought. As they took another stroll on the beach she stopped, put her arms around him, and kissed him. Then just took his hand and walked on. *Maybe the subtle approach would be more seductive*, she pondered that thought as they walked. They talked of past relationships and expectations of new ones. She needed to find out more about his past experience so she would understand his hesitation. As they entered the hotel room, he stopped and told her once again how much he enjoyed their time together that day and kissed her. She reciprocated with a warm response. While she was changing clothes, he walked out onto the balcony of their suite. *Sabrina is a very beautiful and loving person. Maybe I just could fall in love with her. After all, we do have a lot in common.* Sabrina joined Brock on the balcony. Watching the waves crashing on the shore with a glorious full moon, he put his arm around her and drew her close. She snuggled against him, and he kissed her again more passionately. As they went inside, they knew their relationship was taking a different turn.

"Well Sabrina, before we take this any further, I think I'll turn in. See you in the morning."

Sabrina tried to cover her shock as best she could.

"Certainly, Brock, it's been quite a day. I'm getting tired as well."

Tossing and turning most of the night as the morning approached, Sabrina realized she was actually falling in love with Brock. She wasn't expecting her feelings for him to go in this direction. It wasn't in her plans. She'd have to get control again. There was no room for 'feelings' in this project. But since he was falling into her plan, she now had to change her approach. Now she knew what it would take.

"Henry, I'm so glad you are getting better, Frank said. "But at your age, you should really be preparing a will; that is, if you haven't already."

"I've had one for years, Frank, but I've recently made some changes in it. It always pays to keep things updated."

"It's sure does, Henry. Especially with the business. It

won't run itself if anything happens to you. I would imagine you've made plans for that."

"Yes, Frank I have, and I'm sure you'll be pleased with what I've set forth in my will."

"We've been partners for a long time Henry, I'm sure you have the best interest of the company at heart. I've been a good partner for you and when the time comes, I'm ready to do my part in making it a more successful company."

"I'm sure you will Frank and I'm counting on your loyalty to the company. We'll have to sit down one day soon and have a long chat, but I'm getting quite tired right now, so I think I'll go to my den and take a brief nap before the news comes on."

"Okay, Henry, I can see myself out."

Wow, maybe Henry is going to put me in his will after all and give me the company. Rightfully so, since I've been his right-hand man for nearly 25 years. Who else would be qualified to handle this company? I know every detail about it.

CHAPTER 13

As Sabrina and Brock landed back in Nashville, they said their goodbyes and headed for their cars.

"See you back at work tomorrow, Brock. It was great being with you this weekend."

"Thanks for all the planning and arrangements you made. It was a fabulous weekend."

As Brock drove off, he knew he did have feelings for Sabrina. However, he really missed Janice. Her friendship really meant a lot to him. He decided he'd text her to see if she'd meet him for coffee in the morning before work.

Since Sabrina had to pass the office on her way home, she decided to stop there. Bob was there working on some paperwork.

"How'd your weekend go, Sabrina?"

"It couldn't have gone better. Well maybe a little better, but he's really coming around. It shouldn't be long until I have him where we want him," she said.

"Good job, Sabrina! This weekend should have done something with the expense and extravagance of it," Bob said as they high fived.

"I think you should do something special for him, Bob, just so he still knows he's doing a good job. The more he feels your approval, the more he feels part of the company. His birthday is coming up. Maybe we should do an office party and you could give him an extra little gift in a card."

"Good thought. I'll get the plan in action."

"His birthday is next Friday."

As the week passed, Bob made plans. When Friday arrived, Bob surprised Brock with a catered lunch. All the sales staff were invited. It was a festive occasion, and as the two-hour lunch wound down, Bob not only presented Brock with a card and check for $10,000, but he also promoted Brock to Senior Executive Sales Manager. Brock was flabbergasted. It was a total surprise.

"We just want to make sure you are taken care of and happy to be here at Justice Medical."

"I don't know what to say, Bob. I certainly didn't expect this. Justice is the best company in the world. Who wouldn't want to be part of such a successful company?"

"Well, we have to give you a lot of credit, Brock. You've

been a great asset here."

Sabrina approached Brock, "I'm so proud of you. Bob is right. You are a great asset here."

"Did you know about this, Sabrina?"

"No, I swear I didn't know what Bob had planned. It was as much of a surprise to me as it was to you. But you deserve it, Brock."

As the party ended, they packed up everything, and said their goodbyes. Brock told Sabrina he'd talk with her later. As he was heading home, he called Janice to tell her about the party. She said she was cooking dinner if he'd like to come by. So, he decided to go by her house on the way home. They had a relaxing evening, sitting on the deck eating, listening to music, and talking.

"This is great Janice, just what the doctor ordered!" They both laughed and enjoyed the rest of the evening. They agreed to have coffee at their favorite coffee shop the next morning. As he left, he realized Sabrina had called a couple of times and left a message for him to call her. He was beat so he thought he'd call her tomorrow.

The next morning Brock headed to the coffee shop to meet Janice, and realized he was sort of excited to be with her. They talked for a couple of hours and decided to head out to The Cowboy Grill that evening since it had been such a long time since they'd been there. He went home and got his guitar out and brushed up on his singing. *Man, it's been too long. I really enjoy playing and singing. This will be fun going tonight with Janice.* As he was singing, his phone rang. He saw it was Sabrina. *I should take her call since I planned to call her back. I'll just text her in a few minutes to let her know I'm really busy and will call her soon.* She left another message. As he listened to her message, she asked if he was ignoring her, and told him to call. *Guess I should call.* He turned on the radio and sat down in his recliner to call her.

"This is WHOW breaking news...country music star Carter Standish has died. More to come on the 5:00 news."

Wow that's terrible. She was a rising country star. Wonder what happened, Brock thought.

"Hi Sabrina, sorry I missed your call. I've been trying to catch up around here. What's up?"

"Well, that's good to hear I thought you might be ignoring me. I've tried several times to reach you."

"I know, just wasn't at a place I could answer, sorry. Do you want to come over for dinner this evening?"

"Oh man, I can't tonight. I have plans with a friend."

"Oh well, maybe we can get together tomorrow."

"Yeah, that might work. Okay, then I'll talk with you tomorrow."

"Hey, wait, did you hear that Carter Standish died?"

"Umm who's that," Sabrina replied.

"You don't know who she is?"

"Umm, no. Should I?"

"She's a rising country music star."

"I really don't like country music. Do you?" Sabrina asked.

"Yes, I kinda do."

"Oh," she said. "Well, got to run, I'll talk with you later, Brock."

As Brock hung up, he started thinking about his and Sabrina's relationship and wondered if they really had anything in common besides work. Later, Brock picked up Janice and told her about Carter Standish. She was shocked to find out Carter had passed away.

"There's been too many people dying young these days," she said.

As they made their way through the Nashville traffic to The Cowboy Grill, laughing and talking as they went along, Brock realized how much they had in common. Their relationship was different, more intimate and personal than the one he had with Sabrina. Entering The Grill, several people came up to them and said how much they missed them and encouraged them to come back more often. Brock signed up to sing and got them something to eat. There were a lot of singers that night. Brock didn't get to sing until 10, but he was really enjoying being there with Janice. The response of the crowd overwhelmed Brock.

"Brock, you just don't know how good you really are!" Janice said, smiling at him.

They went to the car after talking to several people at the close of the evening. As he drove Janice home, he realized how much he had missed their time together and how much he relaxed just being with her.

"Thanks, Janice, for encouraging me to go back to The Grill. It really was fun. I felt a little rusty singing at first, but I guess the crowd didn't notice," Brock said with a laugh.

"Oh Brock, you were wonderful as usual," Janice said smiling. "I had a great time. Thanks for coming tonight. It's been too long."

"I have to agree with you there, Janice." Brock looked at her and realized how fond he was of her.

CHAPTER 14

The next morning Sabrina called. Brock woke up from a sound sleep at the ring of his phone. He looked at it, saw it was Sabrina, laid it down, and went back to sleep. She called back later to arrange a time for their dinner Saturday evening. Brock had promised to go but wasn't enthusiastic about it. They spent the evening together, but Sabrina knew there was something not quite right.

"Are you okay Brock? You seem to be a little distant this evening. A little distracted."

"Yes, I'm fine, Sabrina. Guess I'm just a little tired."

Monday morning rolled around, and Brock got to work earlier than usual. As he got into the elevator, he decided to go to the lab since everyone seemed to be too busy to take him there. He got off the elevator and made his way back to the lab on the main floor. The lab was at one end of the facility, and he noticed that there was an extra set of doors before he got to the lab. As he opened the second set of doors, he ran into two security guards. He was shocked to see them. Brock told them who he was, and they said he didn't have clearance to be there. He was surprised that clearance was necessary, but figured with the formulation for *Milagro*, that it probably was a good thing. It's been such a successful product, and the patents are still pending.

"Fine," he said, "I'll get with Bob soon and I'm sure he'll give me a tour."

He got back on the elevator and headed to his office. *This is going to be a busy week, training six new sales reps.* He arrived at his office and found Sabrina waiting for him.

"Good morning, Brock, I stopped by the coffee shop on my way up and brought us coffee and a pastry to start our busy day."

"Aww, thanks for being so thoughtful, Sabrina. It is going to be a hectic week again. *Milagro*'s sales have certainly accelerated! It's one of the hottest products on the market! I'm surprised the lab can keep up with the expansion. Have you been down there?"

"No, I haven't."

"Maybe we could go together sometime," Brock said. "I'd love to see it."

"Sure, Brock, one of these days when we get some time," Sabrina replied. "Well, have to get to my office, see you later, Brock."

On her way to her office, she stopped at Bob's office and told him about Brock wanting to see the lab. Bob was concerned that it was the second time he'd brought that up.

"We need to step up our game, Sabrina. If he finds out, we could be in big trouble. We need to make sure he's in so deep he can't get out."

"I know, Bob. We're almost there."

"Don't let me down, Sabrina. A lot is riding on this."

"Believe me, I know, Bob."

Frank was leaving the office for the day when he ran into Sabrina coming out of Bob's office. He decided to check to see why she was there.

"Hey Bob, what's she doing up here?"

"Oh, hello Frank. Uh, well, I asked her up here to see how her sales were going. A little personal touch never hurts."

"Well don't make it a practice. There's something about that girl that just rubs me the wrong way."

"I know, Frank, but just leave it to me I like to stay in touch with those who want to climb the ladder, you know, keep an eye on them."

"Okay, I hope you know what you're doing."

"I do. Anything else you need?"

"No, I was just getting ready to check on Henry. He hasn't been feeling well again."

"Oh really? Bob said. I hope he doesn't have the flu again."

"No, I'm not sure what's going on. He seems to be a little disoriented. But I guess when you get to be his age, you never know what may happen," Frank said.

"He's been in fairly good health until just recently though," Bob responded. "Maybe I'll go see him, too."

"Oh, you don't have to do that. I'll keep you informed. When you get to be 89 you've lived a long life and can expect a few rough bumps. Too bad he doesn't have any living relatives."

"Yes, too bad," Bob said with a chuckle under his breath. "Well, let me know how he's doing this evening when you leave."

"Alright, sure thing, Bob."

As Frank walked out to his car, he couldn't wait to see how Henry was doing. Maybe the 'medicine' he was giving him was working better this time. As Frank pulled up to Henry's house, he noticed a neighbor coming out.

"Excuse me ma'am, can I be of any assistance," Frank asked.

"Oh, I was just making sure everything was okay at

Henry's house since the rescue squad took him to the hospital this morning."

"What? Oh no, what happened?"

"Well, I went to check on him since he hasn't been feeling well. I made some chicken soup for him. You know how that settles your stomach when you're sick. They tell me I make the best chicken…"

Frank interrupted her, "Enough about that, what happened to Henry?" Frank said agitatedly.

"Well, you don't have to get huffy; I was getting to that! He just didn't look good, you know his coloring was off, so I thought I'd better call 911. I'm sure they must know by now what's wrong with him so I'm planning on going to the hospital soon. Where are you going so fast, mister?"

Frank jumped into his car and took off to the hospital. *I hope they haven't finished testing him yet. This could be disastrous!* As he was arriving at the hospital, he noticed some police cars there. *Maybe I'd better make other arrangements just in case.* So, he sped off to his house, stopping to get gas along the way. After he arrived, Frank checked his house to make sure everything was okay. He got his credentials and threw some clothes and toiletries in his new rolling duffle bag. He put it in a laundry bag just in case someone was watching his house, he didn't want to give them any reason to be suspicious. As he left his house, he decided to call the hospital to check on Henry. They said there wasn't anyone there by that name. He must still be in the emergency room. So, he swung by Henry's house to see if he could find the will again. As he approached the house, he noticed the police had just arrived. He pulled over to the curb to watch before he got any closer.

Frank needed to cover his tracks. He called Bob and told him that he had decided last week to go see his sister in California but forgot to tell him he was going, and he'd be back in a couple of days. It had been a while since he'd seen her. She has been sick, and this was the only chance he had for a while, he said. Bob thought that was kind of sudden, but if his sister was sick, he should go. Frank had already made some plans in case he needed to get out of town quickly. He decided to drive to Memphis then book a flight to Cancun. It was a long flight going through Atlanta, but that's the best he could do for now. *Good thing I've been stashing away some cash for a rainy day and those new credit cards will come in handy as well!* He decided to call Bob back to tell him he saw Henry, and he wasn't up to par but was doing okay. He didn't want Bob to become suspicious. *This really isn't going like I'd planned. Why couldn't that nosey neighbor mind her own business! I would have been sitting pretty, owner of Justice Medical in just a month or two. I should have organized a plan B better, but it's too late for that. I just hope I got a good head start on the police.*

CHAPTER 15

The next evening, Henry succumbed to his illness. As the day progressed and the police investigation began, they were able to locate Henry's will, and found that he was leaving all his personal and professional interests, including Justice Medical, to his daughter. He left his house to Frank. They spoke with Bob Baker first and told him what had happened. He was in shock that Henry had passed away and that it was a suspicious death. They asked about Frank Callahan. Bob told them of his trip to California, but that he'd be back in a couple of days. He knew Frank would be devastated to hear the news because he'd just looked in on him before he left yesterday. Henry had seemed all right. The police inquired of others that were close to Henry. Bob didn't know of anyone because of Henry's age. Most of his friends had already passed. The investigator thanked him for his time. Then asked if they could talk to Henry's daughter. Bob nearly fell off his chair, he didn't know anyone knew about her.

"His daughter?"

"Yes, she works here, Sabrina Carpenter."

"Oh, yes. Yes, she does. I'm not sure she knows of his demise yet."

He called Sabrina and asked her to come to his office. She was overwhelmed when she found out about Henry's death.

"Please, officer, I need to sit down, and could you get me a glass of water?"

She looked at Bob and was obviously shaken. The police asked about their relationship.

"I searched for him when I found out he was my father. I didn't really get to know him. I just wanted to get to know his business and then get to know him. I understand that he spent a lot of time building up this business. I wish I had gotten to know him first now. I thought I had plenty of time. How did he die? Was he ill?"

"Ms. Carpenter, we suspect foul play."

"What?! I can't imagine anyone wanting him dead."

"Actually, Ms. Carpenter, you are the one to gain the most from his death."

"What do you mean?"

"Ms. Carpenter, you are the main beneficiary of his will."

She could hardly speak, "What? Certainly you aren't saying I had anything to do with this, are you?"

"Well, we would like you to come to the precinct for some questioning."

"Bob, tell them I had nothing to do with this! No! No!"

"Please Ms. Carpenter, you can come willingly, or we can handcuff you."

"Okay, I'll go but I want you to know it wasn't me! I hardly knew him."

As they left, Brock came to Bob's office and saw them take her out.

"What's going on, Bob? Where are they taking Sabrina?"

"Sit down, Brock. Henry Justice has died, and they suspect foul play."

"I'm sorry to hear that, but what does that have to do with Sabrina?"

"No one knows this, Brock, but she's Henry's daughter by a mistress he had while working in California."

Brock was stunned, "How long has she known about him?"

"Only about two and a half years. She arrived here looking for a job. We hired her, and while I was working with her, she slipped up and mentioned something about her father here. Then she ended up telling me who she was. But no one knows, not even Frank. I promised I wouldn't tell anyone. But this certainly upsets the apple cart now, doesn't it?"

When Brock left the office, he swung by Janice's house and told her what happened.

"I'm so sorry Brock. I can see you are overwhelmed with the news."

Since it was late in the day, she decided to turn on the local news to see if they could learn more. While waiting for the news, she finished cooking the dinner she had begun before he arrived. As they began to eat, the news came on, but it didn't give them any further information. He stayed for a while since he felt so at home at her place.

"Please keep me informed, Brock. A death is upsetting, but for it to be suspicious, especially at his age, is even worse."

"I will, Janice, and thanks for always being there for me."

Man, am I tired, Frank thought on the flight. *Driving three hours and now a six-hour flight to Cancun is exhausting. But at least I'm on my way out of Nashville.*

I'm really glad I thought to have two alternate IDs. Those credit cards will be a lifesaver as well. I don't have as much in my bank account in Cancun as I'd like, but at least I have something. Hopefully, they won't find me there. I need to plan my last leg of the trip from Cancun. After he arrived in Cancun, he found a place to stay and checked in. *I feel like I could sleep for two days,* he thought to himself as he got into the bed. *I'm too old for this gallivanting all over creation! But I guess you do what you gotta do. Tomorrow I'll start planning the last leg of the trip, but I'll stay here for a few days. London sounds like a good place to blend in for a while. Then maybe go to Italy, who knows? We'll see what tomorrow brings.*

"Detective, I've told you everything I know," Sabrina said with a frustrated tone in her voice.

"Well, maybe we should lock her up until she decides to give us the lowdown."

"You can't do that," Sabrina said as she pounded the table. "I should have asked for an attorney sooner. I need to call my lawyer!"

"Let her make the call."

Sabrina called her attorney, Jake Turnour. Jake is one of the most prominent attorneys in Nashville, specializing in corporate law. As she talked to her lawyer, he was shocked to hear what had happened. He assured her that she didn't have anything to worry about but said she should have called him sooner.

"I know, but I knew I didn't do anything wrong. I didn't think it would go this far! They are trying to pin this on me, Jake!"

"I'll be right there, Sabrina. Don't say another word!"

After Frank hadn't called in two days, Bob tried to call him. He kept getting voicemail. *I guess he must be on the plane coming home. I'll give him until tomorrow to call or come in, but then I'm calling his sister. I know I've got her name and number written down somewhere.*

"How's everything going, Bob? I haven't heard from Sabrina," Brock said.

"She's still at the precinct," replied Bob. "She's had a pretty rough day. They're trying to pin this death on her because no one else has a motive. The autopsy should be back in a few weeks. You know, sometimes it can take up to three months or longer to get it back. I guess they will do a cremation and then have the funeral later. We won't know the cause of death until the autopsy report is back."

"They really believe someone tried to kill the poor old man? Why would anyone want to do that? He wasn't bothering a soul," Brock said.

"I don't know. I hope they are mistaken. I'm sure the autopsy won't show anything. I can't believe it would, considering he was elderly anyway. He was a nice old man with some health problems. I don't know why the police think it's a suspicious case."

As Bob's phone began to ring, Brock excused himself from the office.

"Frank! It's about time you called. I was getting worried."

"Yeah, well my sister is still under the weather so I'm going to stay here a few more days," Frank replied.

"Frank, I've got some bad news."

"What is it, you have a bad golf game?" Frank said with an up-roaring laugh.

"No, it's Henry."

"How is the old man, hope he's feeling better."

"No, Frank, he passed away."

"What? How'd that happen? He was fine the last time I saw him."

"Evidently he took a turn for the worse, or someone tried to kill him."

Frank nearly dropped his phone.

"What do you mean someone tried to kill him?"

"The police think his death is suspicious. They are doing an investigation."

"I can't believe that," Frank replied anxiously. "Who'd have the motive to do that to the old codger? He was a nice elderly man."

"I don't know. I can't imagine. I'm hoping it's a mistake and that the autopsy comes back with 'natural causes' listed as the cause of death," Bob replied.

Yeah, that would be nice, but not likely, Frank thought.

"I'm really sorry to hear about his death," Frank said.

Frank and Bob talked briefly about Henry and the last few months.

"Well Bob I just wanted to touch base with you. Let me know if you hear any more about Henry."

"Alright, Frank. See you in a few days. Tell your sister hello for me, and I hope she's feeling better."

As they hung up, Frank paced nervously. *I've got to figure out another plan faster than I expected. I'm glad I have two identities. I'll have to use this one for a while then change it out. I also need to change my appearance after I leave here. Maybe lose some weight and shave my head. Change my wardrobe, too. I can't be too careful."*

CHAPTER 16

After Jake arrived at the precinct, he was able to talk with Sabrina some more. He told the detective that they didn't have any evidence to hold Sabrina any longer. He said they had to let her go, and Sabrina was released. Jake took her back to the office to pick up her car and told her to get some rest and he'd talk with her tomorrow. Bob was still there so she talked with him for a while then went home. After she got something to eat, she called Brock to tell him all that had happened and how scared she was, since she'd never been through anything like that. She asked Brock to come over the next evening for dinner. Brock said he couldn't because he'd made plans with a friend. Maybe he could come the following evening.

After they hung up, Brock called Janice to make sure they were still on for The Grill. She confirmed they were. After he hung up with Janice, his phone rang. It was Carrie. Should he answer or just let it ring? He let it ring. He had no interest in talking with her. She called back about an hour later, and he was tempted to let it ring again, but he thought something might be wrong since he hadn't heard from her in over a year.

"Carrie, what do you want?"

"Well, Brock, is that any way to answer the phone! After all, we haven't talked in a while."

"Yeah, hasn't it been nice?" Brock said with a chuckle.

"Brock! I was just calling to see how you are and if things are working out for you in Nashville."

"Yes, everything is great. Work is great, I have some new friends. Couldn't be better. Now if that's all you want, I'll hang up now." Click.

"Brock! Brock?"

Well, that jerk! I thought he would be glad to talk to me. Maybe even miss me a little. I had to find out before I got serious with Marty. He is a really nice guy, but I guess I'll always have a special place in my heart for Brock. But the main thing with Marty is he has a really great job as the CEO of Glass Financials. He's a great catch, and I won't have to worry about my finances anymore! she thought with a big grin. *Yes, he must be the one I've been waiting for and that is why the others haven't worked out.*

As the investigation continued into Henry's cause of death, they began checking into Justice Medical to see if anyone else had a motive. They had already found a copy of Henry's will at his house. The detectives had noticed that Henry had left his house to Frank but decided that wasn't enough motive to kill someone. They also noticed that sales with the company had soared in the past couple of years, especially in the last year. Further investigation revealed a new product development of a popular weight loss system called *Milagro*. They decided to talk with Frank Callahan. After arriving at the company, they realized he wasn't back from visiting his sister, as Bob had told them. So, they got his cell number and tried to call to no avail.

"I'm sure if you try again later," Bob said, "he'll answer. He's probably just taking care of his sister."

So, they thanked Bob for his time. The investigator tried a little while later with no answer, this time leaving a message for him to call them back. After Frank got the message, he realized who had called him since he didn't recognize the number. *Now what should I do? I can't call them back. They might realize where I am. Maybe if I got one of those disposable phones, and stopped using my phone then they couldn't track the call. Yes! That's what*

I'll do and take the battery out of my phone. Brilliant!
"Sometimes I amaze myself," he said with a chuckle. He
got in his car and went to one of the local stores and bought
a couple of phones. After returning home and setting up
one of those phones, he called the investigator and told
them that he was sorry he missed their calls, but his phone
wouldn't keep a charge, and he had to buy a phone to call
them. He didn't want to keep them waiting. He'd have to
get a new phone when he got back to town in a few days.
His sister was still under the weather but was improving
some. The investigator asked him about the recent increase
in sales. He explained about the new weight loss system.

"People love a product that makes weight loss easy,"
he said.

He hoped he was giving all the right answers to make
sure the investigator was satisfied.

"Have you got the autopsy back yet?" Frank asked.

The investigator said they hadn't but expected it within
a couple more weeks.

"I should be back before the funeral. I wouldn't miss
that for the world. He was such a nice man and we worked
closely together for nearly 25 years."

He had to throw off any suspicion.

"Anything else I can help you with, detective?"

"No, I think that's all for now. Thanks for returning my call."

"Sure thing, detective."

Whew! Got through that one. I better call Bob and follow up with him about my phone just to cover my bases. They talked for about five minutes. Just enough relaxed conversation so Bob wouldn't be curious, including talking about the great California weather.

Brock and Janice had another great time at The Grill.

"Brock, you know they love you at The Grill. You get better and better the more you sing. You're even getting pretty relaxed on stage. I love to hear you sing."

"Janice, I think you're my biggest fan!"

"Of course I am!"

"Thanks for the encouragement. I used to want to make this my career but didn't think I could make a living at it."

"Brock, I bet if a talent scout was listening to you, you'd have a contract in a heartbeat."

"Oh, I don't know about that."

"You are just being modest. You are really good! I mean it!"

As they arrived back at Janice's house, while sitting in the car, Brock realized how relaxed he was around her, and how much he appreciated her. He just shook his head and smiled, thinking, *I could get used to this.* Suddenly Brock realized his feelings for Janice had grown deeper.

"What are you smiling about, Brock?"

"Oh nothing."

"Come on, what is it?"

"I was just thinking how much I enjoy your company."

"Well, I like being with you too, ole friend!"

They smiled at each other. *If he knew how I really felt,* she thought. "Guess I'll go on in, it's getting late."

"Yes, I'd say 1:30 a.m. is a little late."

They laughed.

"You want to meet for coffee in the morning, not early though?" she said with a laugh.

"Sure, let's meet around 10 at our, umm, the coffee shop."

"Okay," she said and smiled as she got out of the car. "No need for you to walk me to the door, Brock. You probably couldn't get out of the car with that swelled head of yours after tonight's performance and how the crowd, umm, the girls, swooned over you!" she said lightheartedly.

He picked up a piece of paper, wadded it up, and threw it at her, laughing. She closed the car door while laughing at him. After watching her walk to the door and close it behind her, he drove off smiling at her remark. *She really is fun to be with, and I love being around her,* he thought. *We have a great time together every time we go out.* As he turned up the radio, singing along with it, the station announced a breaking story, "Further details in the morning on the 6:00 a.m. news on WHOW, where you hear it first." *Wonder what happened*, he thought. *I'm sure I won't be up at 6:00 a.m. he chuckled.*

CHAPTER 17

As the investigation continued, they delved further into the company Henry Justice owned. There seemed to be something more to this weight loss system than first thought. It seemed people were buying more and more of it, like it was an addiction.

"I think we need to talk to Brock Morgan. He seems to be the main salesperson for this line at Justice," the detective decided.

On Monday morning Brock arrived at work. He finished up his last sales training as the detective arrived.

"Can we speak to you, Mr. Morgan?"

"Sure thing, what's on your mind, detective?"

"Can you tell us about this weight loss system you are promoting?"

"Yes, as much as I know."

He explained how he'd left Pennsylvania and come to Nashville and applied for the job. His training, who trained him, and the process they used in promoting the products. People tried it, saw results, and loved it. They didn't want to be without it because it was helping their weight, energy, and overall productiveness. It was their miracle product, one person told him.

"Does that strike you as a little strange?" the detective remarked.

"Well, no I guess not. I really haven't thought about it. The sales took off and it's all I could do to keep up. I've worked long hours and sort of haven't had much of a life since I've been here."

The detective thanked him. After going back to the precinct, the detectives called and talked with another employee of the company and found out that Sabrina was Brock's supervisor. The captain at the precinct agreed to put another agent on with them to further investigate some areas in which they needed answers.

"Something just doesn't add up. I have a gut feeling about this, that something just isn't right," the detective said.

The autopsy report came back after four and a half weeks. They had expedited the report because it was being investigated. There were several underlying health issues with Henry that his doctor didn't know about. But there was a trace of something in his body that was suspicious: arsenic.

Detective Brower entered Justice Medical only to see Bob Baker leaving.

"Hold on, Mr. Baker. Can we talk with you for a few minutes?"

"Well," he said, looking at his watch, "I can only give you about five minutes. I'm on my way to an appointment. Let's step into this conference room."

"Mr. Baker, we got the autopsy back on Mr. Justice. There was a trace of arsenic found in his body."

"What?" Bob almost fell back so he sat down on the nearest chair. "You've got to be kidding me!"

"No sir. We wouldn't joke about a matter like this. Would there be any reason why arsenic would be in his body besides someone giving it to him?"

"No, not that I'm aware of. I can't imagine who would kill an old man. He'd probably be gone in a few years anyway. He had been homebound for nearly a year after he finally retired. He couldn't see well enough to drive anymore. He had a few people helping him, like Frank, a neighbor, and I think a homebound service."

"Well, if you think of anything else, please contact us immediately. We'll go see the neighbor. When do you think Frank will be back?"

"Well, I sort of expected him back by now, but certainly before Henry's funeral. Which I'd think would be in the next few days. I'm hoping to hear from him soon. He's having a problem with his phone."

"Yes, he told me that when I talked with him the other day," the detective responded. "So, you don't have a way to reach him?"

"No, but I think I may have his sister's phone number and address somewhere. I've been meaning to look for it and haven't had a chance. I'll try to find it this evening."

"We'd appreciate that. And thanks for your time, Mr. Baker."

"Hi, Sabrina, I'm sorry we weren't able to get together this weekend. Things sure have been hectic."

"Me too, Brock."

"Have the police talked to you anymore?"

"No, why?"

"Well, they questioned me about my job and *Milagro*," Brock said.

"What? Why?"

"I don't know. I think it's just part of their investigation. Can you think of any reason why they'd question me?"

"No! Why did you ask me that?"

"Just curious why they'd talk to me instead of you or Bob, since you all were involved with it way before I was."

"Oh, I see…They're probably questioning everyone that's affiliated with Justice. I don't mean to change the subject, but I was wondering if you'd want to come for dinner this evening, Brock. I've got steaks marinating to cook on the grill."

"Hey, that sounds good. Sure, what time?"

"Around 6:30 p.m."

"Alright, see you then. Sounds great."

Sabrina called Bob immediately.

"Hello Bob, can you talk?"

"Sure Sabrina, what's on your mind?"

"Brock told me today that the detective questioned him about *Milagro*."

"You're kidding me!"

"No, that's what he said."

"What did they want to know?"

"They questioned him about his job and the product."

I can't imagine they are onto anything, Bob thought.

"What reason would they have to look into it?" Bob questioned.

"Brock said it was part of their investigation over Henry's death."

"They did stop me on the way to my meeting this afternoon," Bob said. "They told me the cause of death."

"Which was what?" Sabrina asked.

"It appears there were traces of arsenic in his body."

"What? Why?"

"Apparently someone was trying to get rid of him."

"He was an old man. Oh, how I wish I'd gotten to know my father. I will always regret that," replied Sabrina.

"I know. I'm sorry you didn't too. You know, you just never know about people. I can't imagine who'd do it."

"Me either," she replied. "Well, I won't worry if you don't think there is reason to then. I just wanted to give you a heads up."

"Okay, glad you did. I'll be watching and listening for more information. Talk with you tomorrow."

As they hung up, Bob considered what Sabrina said. He was concerned. He just didn't want Sabrina to be, just in case she'd say something accidentally. *Well, while I'm here in my office at home I should look for Franks sister's number. It's got to be here somewhere.* After looking for half an hour Bob gave up. *Certainly, it has to be at the office if not here. I'll look tomorrow. I can't believe Frank's been gone for almost three weeks. That's not like him. Well, since they have Henry's funeral planned for Saturday, I guess he'll be back by then. I'll call him tomorrow when I hopefully find his sister's number.*

CHAPTER 18

As soon as Bob got to the office the next morning Detective Brower and his new sidekick, Lane Redmond, were there waiting for him.

"And why do I have the honor of your presence so early this morning, gentlemen? Come on into my office and I'll get us a cup of coffee. Have a seat."

"Thanks, but we won't be long, just a few questions."

"Alright, the coffee is ready. Don't you just love these one-cup coffee makers?" Bob said with a chuckle.

"Yes, they are nice and convenient. Thanks for the coffee."

"Okay, what can I do for you?"

"How well do you know Brock Morgan?"

"Well, we spent some time together when we hired him."

"Who is 'we'?" Brower asked.

"Well, I mean when I hired him. 'We' as in the company."

"Have you noticed anything different about him in the last few months?"

"No, I haven't noticed anything, why?"

"We are looking into the product *Milagro*."

"Really?" Bob said, trying to keep his composure by drinking his coffee. "Why are you looking into that?"

"The sales for this product are over the top and we are wondering why."

"What does this have to do with Henry's death?"

"We're not sure yet, but in time we'll know whether it is related. Can you give us some information on the product, Mr. Baker?"

"Well, it was developed as a comprehensive plan. A diet plan with recipes, a pill that helps curb your appetite, and an exercise routine. We tried to make it simple and easy for people to lose weight. It caught on pretty fast as we went to various local places where we knew people were wanting to get into shape and lose weight and then Brock developed a system to put the product online to sell. It really took off then. Any other questions, gentlemen?"

"No, I guess that sums it up for now. Well, thanks for

the coffee. I'm sure we'll talk to you again."

"Sure thing, guys. You have a great day!"

As they left, Bob sat down to try to compose himself. *I need to figure out what to do with the lab. We can't stop production, but maybe we can limit what we have in the lab. I'll go see Gary, to find out his opinion.* Bob waited to make sure the detectives were gone and then went to the lab. He got off the elevator and went to the lab, the security guards greeted him.

"Hi Mr. Baker, nice to see you. Hey, did that fellow Brock get with you about touring the lab? He came down here the other day. I told him he didn't have clearance. He said he'd get with you."

"Oh yeah, I'll catch up with him. Thanks for the info."

Brock is getting a little too persistent on this lab tour, Bob thought. *As long as he doesn't have clearance then he won't be able to get through. I don't have time or the energy to worry about that. I'll deal with him later.*

"Hey Gary, I need to talk with you."

"Let's go to my office," Gary said.

They went to Gary's small office and closed the door.

"Maybe one day you can give me a larger office, Bob," Gary chuckled.

"We don't have time for small talk. The police are investigating Henry's death. They are asking questions about *Milagro*. What can we do to secure our ingredients, if you know what I mean?"

"Wow! Well, let me think a minute," Gary responded. "Maybe if we put one of our ingredients in containers we could transport out of here with some notice, then that might work."

"Well, do what you have to do now that you know it might be investigated, along with everything else. Just let me know what you decide. On second thought, maybe I shouldn't know. Just do it. Thanks, Gary."

"You got it, boss."

As Bob went back upstairs to his office, he stopped by Brock's office to find out how his sales team was producing.

"Hi Bob, come on in and have a seat. How's it going?"

"Okay I guess, just concerned about Henry's investigation. Hey, what's the status of your sales team? How many people do you have working for you now?

"We have a sales crew of 22 people. We're thinking about hiring a few more. Why?"

"Oh, just wondering how this will affect... I mean I'm just wondering how large your team has become with all the success you're having with the weight loss system."

"It is booming, Bob. The progress the sales have made has been quite satisfying to me as well as the team. It's like hitting a gold mine," Brock said enthusiastically. "We are expecting sales to continue to increase this year."

"Well, I just wanted to check in with you, I'm sure you'll continue to do an excellent job to keep things flourishing. Talk with you later."

Hmm, that was kind of peculiar, Brock thought. *Bob seemed somewhat down or distracted and maybe even a little agitated, even while asking about Milagro. Something else must be on his mind, or it could just be Henry's death, knowing someone was responsible for his death. Oh well, I have to get refocused on these sales figures. Maybe before I do that, I'll call Janice to see what she's up to tonight.*

"Hi Brock, good to hear from you. You don't usually call during the day. Something up?"

"No, not really. But I did just have a peculiar visit from Bob a few minutes ago."

"Really? How so?"

"He just wasn't himself, very distracted."

"It could be because of the death of the owner of the company."

"Yeah, I guess you're probably right."

"Oh, by the way," Janice replied. "you know those

mysterious deaths that have been occurring lately? There's been another one. I just heard it on WHOW."

"Really? What'd they say?"

"The same thing, they are investigating it. I would think they would have some idea what's going on. It's getting kind of scary. I wonder if it's random or if they're connected."

"How many have died," Brock said.

"I'm not sure, I think it's been about six now."

"I guess there have been a few I haven't heard of, being so busy here at work," Brock responded. "Hey, I'm getting another call, I'll see you tonight after work if that's okay."

"Sure, Brock, you're welcome anytime."

"Hi, Sabrina, what's up?"

"I was just perusing your sales figures for the last few months. You and your team have really boosted sales significantly."

"Well, where there's a demand...Funny you should contact me now about this, Bob was just in here asking about it."

"Really?" Sabrina said curiously.

"Yes, but he seemed rather distracted. Have you talked

with him lately?"

"Yes, but I didn't really notice anything at the time," said Sabrina. "It's probably nothing. He's got a lot on his mind with Henry's death and all."

"That's what I was sort of thinking as well," Brock said nonchalantly. "You're probably right. I'm going to go for a coffee run. You want something?"

"No thanks," Sabrina replied. "Hey, can I talk with you later? Something just came up."

"Sure, no problem, I'm headed out for coffee now," Brock said.

Then they hung up. *I've got to see what Bob is upset about. I hope it doesn't have anything to do with the investigation. I'm going to talk to him face to face so I can see his expression,* Sabrina thought.

"So, Redmond, what do you think is going on over at Justice Medical?" asked Detective Brower.

"You know, Sam, I don't have a good feeling about this whole thing. Justice's death, astronomical sales suddenly after years of stable increase in sales. But now it's over the top. I think we need to do some investigating into this new product and those involved with it. It appears the product was in a development phase when this 'Brock Morgan' was hired. Then about six months later sales started soaring. I think at the time it appears he was working with Sabrina Carpenter. There's just something fishy about her. I can't put my finger on it, but I will. She's involved with all this somehow."

"I see your point, Redmond. I'll continue my investigation with the death after the funeral tomorrow, and we'll see where that leaves us. You continue your inquiry about this new product, *Milagro*. Keep me updated. I want to blow this thing out of the water if there's something dubious going on. Let's put our diagram up on the board for both of these and see what we have. Okay, it appears that Frank Callahan was the closest to Justice, but no real motive as of now to kill him, but we still need to have a conversation with him. With the funeral being tomorrow, he should be back in town today. So let's make plans to talk with him after the funeral. However, Sabrina Carpenter has motive but claims she didn't have anything to do with it. It doesn't appear she is lying about that, but there's just something in my gut that says she's not on the level. Then there's Baker, he seems to be helpful and genuinely concerned about Justice. Morgan seems to be on the up and up, but he's been in charge of the sales of the new product at Justice. With sales soaring since that came on the market, maybe we should do a little investigation of this new product. Find out where it's made, and who's involved with it. So, let's proceed individually, and see if we can make some progress here."

CHAPTER 19

Bob was in his office finishing some work for the evening when Sabrina knocked on his door.

"Bob, are you busy?" Sabrina asked. "I'd like to speak with you a little more on the *Milagro* inquiry."

"I'm a little busy right now, Sabrina. I'm trying to wrap things up here to go to dinner with some friends."

"Oh," she said a little disappointed. "Then I'll talk with you another time."

She closed the door and went back to her office unsure of what to think. Why was he questioning Brock? *Guess I'll have to wait until I can talk with him again in person so I can see his reactions.*

Just as Bob was getting ready to leave, his phone rang.

"Bob, how's everything going back there?" Frank asked.

"Frank, I figured you'd be back by now. The funeral is tomorrow."

"Oh wow, Bob. You know, my sister has taken a turn for the worse. Has double pneumonia now. I can't leave her. I'm all she has to take care of her. I hate that I won't be at the funeral. Poor ole soul."

"I hate to hear that about your sister, I'm sure you're really worried about her. I hope she gets feeling better soon. She's been sick for a while now."

"I didn't realize how ill she actually was. She didn't want to worry me and all," Frank said with a smirk on his face. "How's the investigation going on Henry's death?"

"They still can't find a motive, but they continue to come by with their questions. They have two investigators on it now."

"Really? Have they said why?" Not caring if Bob had an answer. "I hear my sister moving around. She's in the hospital you know. I need to go. I'll call you again soon."

It seems every time I talk to him something else has changed. This is really worrying me now, Frank thought nervously. *I hope I'm safe with just two ID's. It will take a while before they try to find me so I'm probably safe enough for now.*

All the employees were at Henry's funeral, even the detectives. They remained in the back of the funeral home chapel so they could observe. It seemed Henry was loved by the older employees, but it appeared the younger ones didn't know him well, if at all. After the service, Detective Brower caught up with Bob.

"I hope you're doing okay, Mr. Baker."

"Yes, I cared a lot about the old man. I don't know what will happen to the company now that he's gone. He and Frank worked together for many years before I got involved with the company."

"You don't say," said Detective Brower. "Speaking of Callahan, where is he?"

"I talked with him yesterday and apparently his sister has taken a turn for the worse. Double pneumonia he said. So, he didn't get to return for the funeral."

"Did you ever find the phone number for his sister's place?" asked Brower.

"I looked at my house but didn't see it. I'll look at the office after I get back."

"Could you call me when you find it?" Detective Brower asked.

"Sure thing. I hope I can find it."

"Me too, I really need to talk with him. There's Detective

Redmond over there so I'll talk with you later."

As he walked over to Redmond, he tried to observe those who remained at the funeral home. Most people were just quietly talking.

"Hey Redmond, did you get to do any investigating on *Milagro?*"

"A little bit. It apparently is a weight loss system that uses a meal plan of recipes planned for a month at a time. And there's also a capsule that you take once a day for a month, then you increase the dosage to two pills a day to get over the 'hump' in the weight loss is what I'm understanding. People are saying it's the best thing since sliced bread! Maybe we should try it!" Redmond said with a laugh and patted Brower on the stomach.

"Alright, Redmond, you're pretty funny, but enough with the jokes."

"Who said I was joking?" Redmond said as he continued to laugh.

"Well, maybe we should look into the pill to see what it's made of and find out where it's made."

"Okay, I'll stop by to see Morgan on my way back to the office," said Redmond, but as he was leaving the service, he thought he'd see if Morgan was still at the funeral home.

After looking for a few minutes, he found him talking

to Sabrina Carpenter.

"Hey, Mr. Morgan, could I speak with you for a moment?"

"Yes, just a second."

Redmond stepped back a little so they would have some privacy while talking. Brock wrapped up his conversation with Sabrina then walked over to the detective.

"Alright, detective what can I do for you?"

"I was wondering about the weight loss system your company is producing, can you tell me a little about it? I've just heard bits and pieces."

"Do we have to do this now at the funeral home?" Brock asked with irritation.

"No, but the longer we put it off, the longer it will take to get to the bottom of his death."

"What's the *Milagro* have to do with the investigation?"

"Maybe nothing, but we have to investigate everything."

So Brock explained all he knew about the company and said the capsules for weight loss were made on site at the company in the lab. But if he needed more information, he'd have to talk to Bob Baker, and explained he had never been to the lab. He went there once but he couldn't get in because he didn't have clearance and security guards were posted at the door. He had asked Mr. Baker to show him around because he would like to see the lab since he's sold so much of the product. Bob had promised to take him but they both had been busy and hadn't gone yet.

"Okay then, I'll let Detective Brower know. I think he may be going over there later. Thanks for your time and sorry about the death of the company's owner."

"Yes, me too."

I wonder how it will affect the company, Brock thought.

As he was leaving the funeral home, Redmond took out his phone to call Brower. "Hey Brower, I think we may have hit a jackpot with this *Milagro* stuff. The lab is on site at Justice Medical, but they have security guards at the door of the lab. Maybe we could go over and check it out."

Redmond continued to relay the things that Brock had told him. Detective Brower told Redmond about Mr. Baker calling him about a phone number he needed and after he got that they could go over. He was expecting to hear about the phone number either today or tomorrow.

"Okay then. I'm on my way to get something to eat, then back to the office to see if I can add anything to our diagram and evidence board. See you back there."

As Bob was heading back to his car to leave, he saw Sabrina going to her car.

"Sabrina," Bob called.

As he walked over to her car, he was thinking about the company and what she would do with it now that she owned it, and how that would affect his position.

"So, what's your plan now?"

"I don't have a clue, Bob, but I do know I need to talk to the company's attorney, and mine, for that matter. This is all so sudden. I know we wanted to have more of a stake in the company, but this is more than we anticipated happening. I'm going to have to call the attorneys now," Sabrina surmised. "Have to run. I'll see you back at the office, Bob."

CHAPTER 20

Instead of calling her attorney, Sabrina got in her car and drove straight to her lawyer's office.

"Is Jake in?"

"Let me check to see if he can see you."

"Is he with anyone?"

"No ma'am, but…"

"Then I'll just go on in. Jake?"

"Umm, hello Sabrina. Something wrong?"

"Yes, and no. Well, I just inherited Justice Medical and all of Henry Justice's property, except his house."

"What? How?"

"I'm his daughter."

"What?! Sit down and explain this to me."

"I'll give you the highlights. My mother had an affair with him 30 years ago. I just found out two and a half years ago that he was my father. So, I came here to get to know him, his business, and whatever else I could find out. I didn't tell anyone who I was when I accepted the job at Justice, but in a conversation with Bob Baker, my boss, I slipped up with something I said, and then I told him. He is the only one who knows. However, I guess that Henry knew about me, but my mother didn't want him around since he was married. So that's why I never knew him. I'm not sure what to do with all of this. I just have so many regrets now."

"First, we need to draw a will for a beneficiary for you. Who would you like that to be?"

"Well, let me think. I guess Bob Baker. He's been with the company and a friend since I've been there."

"Anyone else?"

"Brock Morgan, I guess. He's really worked hard since he's been with the company. He deserves it as much as anyone."

"Alright, I'll get started on the documents now and we can set up a meeting with the company attorneys as soon as possible to ensure a smooth transition."

"I knew you'd know what to do to ease my mind. Thanks, Jake! Let me know when all of that is set up. See you soon."

What a relief! Sabrina thought as she left his office. *I need to get to Justice to talk with Bob.* As she drove over, she turned on the radio to listen to some music to try to calm her nerves. A few minutes later a news bulletin came on.

"This is WHOW reporting yet another death of a 34-year-old woman. More details to come when we have them."

Man, there certainly have been a lot of deaths recently. It seems like they are reporting one every couple of weeks. I hope it's not a serial killer! Oh gosh! Maybe I'd better be more careful and watch my surroundings better, Sabrina thought. As she drove to the office, she speculated about the business and what she was going to do with it. *Henry dying, whatever the circumstance, wasn't quite on my radar. It will take some time to get all the legal mumbo jumbo cleared up, but probably in about six months, I will be financially set for life.* With the success of *Milagro*, as she pondered all the implications of her father's death, of getting to know him, and now owning the company, she was conflicted with sadness, yet joyful. *I can't wait to talk to Bob.* As she parked her car, she saw the detectives entering the building. *What do they want now? I'll be glad when this investigation is over. I can't imagine who'd want to harm Henry, but I hope they find them soon!*

The detectives, already in the building and getting on the elevator to go to Bob's office, saw Sabrina approaching and held the elevator for her.

"Hello, gentlemen. Thanks for holding the elevator for me."

Oh, how I wish they'd gone on, she thought.

"How is your investigation coming along?" she asked.

"We're making some progress with it."

"That's good. Hope you find them soon."

"So do we."

The elevator doors opened, and they all stepped out, and headed toward Bob's office.

"Oh, well if you are going to see Bob, then I'll head to my office. I don't want to intrude on your conversation with him," she said.

"Thanks, Sabrina. We appreciate that," Brower said.

Bob saw them coming and greeted them at the door.

"Come on in, detectives. I looked for the phone number, and just found it about five minutes before you arrived. I haven't tried to call, but if you'd like for me to call while you're here, I can."

"No, that won't be necessary. We'll call after we get

back to the station. But we really appreciate your efforts in locating the number. We won't keep you then."

"Anything else I can do for you?"

"No, but I'm sure we'll be in touch."

"We'll see ourselves out."

Redmond was curious as to why Brower didn't inquire about the lab.

"You'll learn, Redmond, that there is a time for everything, and this wasn't the time. I'm going to go back with a warrant. We need to be prepared in case they don't want to show us the lab."

A few minutes later Sabrina came to Bob's office. She asked about the visitors he had and was relieved they only wanted a phone number.

"I saw my attorney and we're setting up a meeting with the company's attorney to get things rolling. I can't believe he left me this company. Doesn't he have any other relatives, Bob?"

"No, he didn't have any children with his wife, and all his siblings are deceased. His wife just passed three years ago."

"Did she know about my mother and me?"

"I don't really know if she did. He kept his personal life

separate from his business life. His wife rarely came here. We saw her at their annual Christmas party for the office, but other than that, she hardly ever came by."

"There's just so much I wish I knew," Sabrina said. "My mother said he was faithful with his support checks after he found out about me."

CHAPTER 21

Back at the precinct, Detectives Brower and Redmond grabbed a cup of coffee and decided to go over the things they had learned about the case. Finishing that, a call was made to Frank Callahan's sister Peg Morehouse.

"Hello, is this Mrs. Morehouse?"

"Yes, it is."

"This is Detective Brower from Nashville."

"Hello, detective."

"Ma'am, how are you feeling?"

"Fine, thank you. Why do you ask, is something wrong?"

"No, ma'am. We were wondering if we could speak to Frank Callahan."

"I'm sorry, he isn't here. Heavens, I haven't seen him in two years! He calls every once in a blue moon, but that's all."

"Really? We were under the impression he was with you."

"No, I haven't seen him, or for that matter, talked to him. I wish he'd stay in touch, but he doesn't. He's all the family I have now."

"Then you wouldn't know how we could find him?"

"No, I'm sorry, detective, I wouldn't have that information. All I know is that he works all the time."

"If he does call or contact you, would you let us know?"

"Certainly, let me get a pen to write your number down. Is he in trouble?"

"No, ma'am. We just need to talk with him."

"Alright, I'll call you if I hear anything."

"Well, that's a strange turn of events," said Brower after handing up. "Where could he be and why? Why would he lie about his sister being ill? Redmond, you get someone to help you make some calls to airlines, trains, etc. to see what you can find out. Looks like maybe we have just had a break in this case. Maybe we should get a search warrant for his house and do some investigation there."

This is the life! Sitting on the beach in Cancun. I think I've covered my tracks pretty well. The diet I've been on has been quite effective. I've already lost ten pounds in two weeks. Another 20, and with the exercise I'm getting, I'll look like a completely different person. Not a bad thing financially, too. Helping me to save some money on food. Another couple of weeks here, then on to London. I think that's a big enough city to blend in for a while, then on to Canada. By then I'll need to get a job. This money won't last forever. I sure do miss Bob. Maybe I'll give the ole guy a call. Even though I enjoy being away and in a tropical climate, I miss work and friends there. Frank was reminiscing as Bob's phone rang at the office.

"Hey Bob, how is everything going back home?"

"Good to hear from you, Frank. It's going pretty well. Henry's funeral was nice. How's your sister doing? She's on the mend, I hope."

"She was released from the hospital two days ago."

"That's good. The detectives wanted to talk with you, so I found your sister's number and gave it to them."

"You did what? I mean, I'll be home soon. Can't they wait till I get home?"

"Sorry, Frank, I guess not. Are you okay?"

"Yes, but it's just been stressful having her so sick, I guess I'm just on edge."

"I thought you sounded pretty good when you called."

"No, not really, I miss being in Nashville, and work. Have you heard anything about what's happening with Justice Medical? Did Henry have a will?"

"Yes, actually he did."

"So what's happening with that?"

"Well, Frank. I guess you should know. He left everything he had to Sabrina Carpenter. She's his daughter by a mistress he had thirty years ago. His only child."

"What! You're kidding right?"

"No, Frank, she got it all. Oh, but the house, Henry left you his house."

You've got to be kidding me! That dump? he thought.

"That's hard to believe," Frank said.

Frank's thoughts got the best of him. *I knew I didn't like that little gold-digger for some reason! She came here so she could get in on Henry's good side, so he'd leave everything to her! I can't believe he didn't leave me anything but the house. We were partners for nearly 25 years!* Frank's anxious thoughts took him down a rabbit trail.

"Frank, are you there?"

"Oh yes, I'm here. Sorry, Bob. I'm just shocked to find out about Sabrina and Henry's will. Anything else I need to know? Anything else going on?"

"No, just the investigation. That's pretty much it. *Milagro*'s still hot. Selling like hot cakes!"

"Well, thanks for the info. Guess I'll go for now, Bob. I'll call you again soon."

As he hung up, he realized he'd have to call his sister to make sure they hadn't called her yet. *That could be a disaster for me,* Frank surmised.

"Hi Peg, it's Frank. Just calling to see how you are since we haven't talked in a while."

"Well, if it isn't my long-lost brother! How are you, Frank? I understand you're supposed to be visiting me," she said with a disgusted chuckle.

"What? Who told you that?"

"Well, a detective called and wanted to speak to you. Asked me how I was doing, too. What are you up to, Frank? Are you in some kind of trouble?"

"No, of course not, Peg," he said with a nervous laugh. "I was planning on coming to see you after my short vacation and I just haven't gotten there yet."

"Well, why would he think I'm sick?"

"I don't know, maybe because you are getting up in age. You know when people are getting older, they have all these aches, pains, and health issues."

"Well, it didn't sound like that to me, Frank! Anyway, he wanted me to call him if I heard from you."

"Oh, don't do that! I mean I'll be back in Nashville soon and I'll contact them when I get back. It's probably about my boss's death. You know how it is when they find somebody dead, they have to investigate it. He was old and just died of old age."

"Are you sure about that Frank?" she asked suspiciously.

"Sure, I mean what else could it be?" Frank said trying to reassure her.

"Well, if you say so. Did you say you were coming for a visit?"

"Well, I'd planned to, but if they need to talk to me, I should get back home. Oh by the way, I had to get one of those disposable phones because mine died on me. I have to get a new one, another reason why I need to get back home."

"Okay then, call me when you get back to Nashville."

"Okay, Peg I will."

Now what am I going to do? Frank thought. *They know I'm not at my sister's house. I guess Bob didn't know or he'd have said something when I called him. Maybe I should call the detective to cover my tracks. Yes, that's what I'll do right now.*

"Hello, may I speak to Detective Brower?"

"Detective Brower, you have a call on line two."

"Brower here."

"Hi Detective, I understand you need to speak to me. This is Frank Callahan."

Brower looked at Redmond and put his hand over the receiver, "This is Callahan! See if you can trace this call."

"Yes, Mr. Callahan. It appears we've got some conflicting information on you. We called your sister to talk with you and found out you weren't there and hadn't been there. Do you have an explanation for us? Your sister said she hasn't seen you in two years!"

"Oh, that poor girl," Frank said. "She has some dementia, and after being so sick it appears it's gotten worse. I decided to take a couple of days rest before I came back there. So I decided to go to the beach. But it looks like I may have to either go back there now or find someone to take care of her since I can't move there. Oh, how distressing." Frank tried his best to sound upset.

"She didn't sound like she had dementia. As a matter of fact she sounded pretty healthy," Brower said.

"No sir, she's not, but she tries her best to be independent. I know I'll have a fight on my hands when I try to put her in a nursing home. She's 80 years old you know. Is there something you needed to ask me detective?"

"Yes, actually. I understand you saw Henry the day before he died. Did he seem ill to you then?"

"Yes, but not unusually so. He'd been sick a lot lately. His age and everything."

"It appears someone was trying to speed up his death."

"What do you mean detective?"

"The autopsy revealed he had traces of arsenic in his body."

"Arsenic?"

"Yes, do you know if anyone would want him dead?"

"Henry? Of course not! He was a nice old man. We were partners for 20+ years. I can't imagine anyone doing that."

After a few more questions, Redmond entered the room and said they were still working on getting a trace and that Frank was talking on a burner phone.

"By the way, where are you staying at the beach? My family and I are thinking of going to California and we are looking for a good place to stay."

"I, umm well, I'm just staying here and there as I'm traveling. No special place just wherever I decide to stop."

"Frank, if you see someplace nice let me know when I see you because we can use all the help we can get in locating a place to stay and a good beach. It's a special vacation for us."

"Sure will, Detective, and if that's all you need, I'll be going so I can get back on the road. Have a good day."

Then he hung up. *I was on there longer than I wanted to be. I hope they didn't trace my phone call! That's all I need!*

Detectives Brower and Redmond continued their investigation into the morning hours. They decided they'd call it a day and start again fresh in the morning. The next day they decided to look closer into *Milagro* by going to the lab, and into Frank's house as well. However, they wanted to get a search warrant for both places before they went, just to be on the safe side. They put off looking into both places for a day so they could get the warrants.

"I think we will benefit by taking a closer look into both those places. There has to be a reason for Frank being gone as long as he has. I'm not so sure about his story on his sister either. He's been gone for almost a month. Maybe we should ask Bob if he's ever done anything like this before we go to the lab."

After they got the warrants the following day, they returned to Justice Medical. The detectives went to see Bob and inquired about Frank's absence from his job. Bob confirmed he'd never been away for more than two weeks, but that these were unique circumstances with his sister. The detectives looked at each other, but it didn't arouse any suspicion with Bob.

"Bob, we'd like to take a look at your lab, if you don't mind."

"They are mighty busy down there. Our standard procedure is to make an appointment with the lab before touring," Bob replied, hoping to delay them for a while.

"Our time is limited, Bob, and if you're unwilling to take us there..." he reached into his coat pocket and pulled out the warrant, "we can use this to go there now."

Bob tried not to show his anxiety and concern.

Trying to cover, he jokingly said, "Now fellas, you don't have to go to that extreme. Let me call to make sure our lab supervisor is there so he can give you the tour."

"Hello, Gary. Bob here. I've got a couple of detectives here that would like to come to the lab for a tour. Do you have a few minutes to show them around?"

"You're kidding right, Bob?" Gary asked. "Okay, cleaning up now and getting our container out of here. Give me at least five minutes."

"Let me check, Gary," as he looked and smiled at the detectives.

"Five minutes okay with you detectives? He's in the

middle of something," Bob said. Brower nodded.

"Okay, we'll see you in a few, Gary."

"Well, Harold, here's what we've been planning for. Clear out the product and go," Gary said.

So, Harold put the lid on the product, and headed for the door to take it out to the car as fast as he could. *No evidence here under my watch*, Gary thought as he wiped off the counter where the preparations were being made.

"Can I get you guys a cup of coffee as we wait?" Bob asked the detectives.

"No thanks. We're glad you're cooperating with us, Bob."

"No problem. We are usually so busy in the lab, and it's rather small for the production we have. Any extra people around sort of disrupts the flow of things."

They continued to make small talk as they waited.

"Well, it's been five minutes so I guess we can head down there."

As they got off the elevator and went to the lab, the security guards greeted them as they entered the double doors.

"Security guards, huh?" Redmond said.

"Yes, you can't be too careful these days," Bob said

with a nervous laugh.

As he opened the door, he looked at Gary. Gary nodded with an all clear. Bob was relieved, to say the least. They walked around and Gary gave them an explanation as to the manufacturing of the product and the distribution. All things considered, the detectives seemed to be satisfied with what they saw and thanked them for the tour and left.

CHAPTER 22

Brower and Redmond got back to the office, grabbed a cup of coffee, and once again looked over the information they had. Brower leaned back in his chair and propped his feet up on his desk. Redmond looked up from the paperwork he was reading. As he was getting ready to ask Brower a question, he noticed something on the sole of Brower's shoe.

"What's that on your shoe, Brower?"

"What do you mean?"

"Looks like you must have stepped on something."

Brower took off his shoe to look at it, and it looked like he had stepped in something white. Some white powder seemed to be lodged in the crevice of his sole.

"Hmmm. Looks like some sort of powdery substance," Brower said. "Let's send it to the lab and find out what it is."

So, they scraped it out of Brower's shoe and bagged it, labeled it and Redmond took it to the lab.

"They said it would take a few days to get the results back," Redmond said as he returned to the office.

"You know Redmond, we should go take a look at Callahan's house. Since he's been gone so long, we might find something we've missed in this investigation."

"Yes, and I think we need to take a look at the Justice house as well. Let's go there first, then over to Callahan's."

When they pulled up in the driveway of Henry Justice's house, they saw a neighbor look out the window.

"I guess she must keep an eye on the neighborhood," Brower said with a laugh.

"Maybe we should talk to her after we're finished, or maybe before. Might just save us some time!"

"Sounds like a plan," said Redmond.

As they got out of their car the neighbor came out of her house.

"Can I help you gentlemen with something?"

"Hello, ma'am. We are Detectives Brower and Redmond."

"Hello, I'm Margie Wakefield."

"We are investigating the death of Henry Justice."

She gasped, "Really? Oh my, he was such a nice man. So kind and thoughtful."

"You knew him pretty well?"

"Yes, we used to talk some after his wife died and he stopped working so much."

"Did you see anything suspicious the day of his death?"

"I went to visit him, as I usually do, he'd been under the weather lately and had been in the hospital after he had the flu. Anyway, he didn't look very good. His coloring was off. So, I called the emergency medical service, and they took him to the hospital. About the middle of the afternoon, I was going out to get the mail, and a gentleman came to visit him. I told him Henry wasn't home and they'd taken him to the hospital that morning. He got all huffy and rude and got in his car and left. I'm glad he didn't come back."

The detectives looked at each other.

"Did you get his name?"

"No, he took off too fast."

"Do you think, ma'am, we could go look around in Henry's house?"

"Of course, detectives. I have a key. Let me get it."

As she went inside to get the key, they walked around

the house looking to see if there was anything out of place. When she arrived with the key, they went inside.

"No reason for you to stay, ma'am. We will be here for a while."

She reluctantly left them to do their job. They took their time looking through his medicine cabinet, dresser drawers, closets, all his clothes, all the cabinets in the kitchen and bathrooms, even in the crevices of the furniture. Even though the house was in somewhat of a disarray, they couldn't find anything wrong. As they were leaving Margie came out.

"Anything else I can help you with, Detectives?"

"No, ma'am," Brower said, "but if we need you, we'll be in touch."

She watched them as they left and then she went to Henry's house to make sure the door was locked. The next stop for the detectives was Frank Callahan's house. On the way there they stopped to get a sandwich at a fast-food chain.

"I can't believe this place stays as busy as it does, but their chicken sandwich is the best around."

They drove on to Callahan's place as they ate. As they pulled up to his house, they noticed the blinds were all closed. They searched around his house for a key. They didn't find one, but finally found a window unlocked at the back of the house. So, Redmond decided to climb in the window and let his partner in the back door.

"Good thing these windows are low to the ground and oversized," Redmond said as he climbed through.

They started their search with the kitchen and went through the entire house, looking through cabinets, drawers, closets, and under furniture before Brower spotted a small bottle on the mantel of the fireplace behind a book.

"Bingo, Redmond! I think we may have found something."

There was one half of a small tablet left in the bottle. They put it in a bag and labeled it for the lab to run their tests. As they left, they locked the door behind them, feeling certain this was another break they needed in the case. When they got back to the precinct, they immediately took the bag to the lab. While down there, Brower inquired about the white powder that had been stuck to his shoe. They hadn't finished all the tests on it yet, but they should be completed within the next couple of days. As the detectives decided to call it a day, they added more information to their evidence board so they could go over it tomorrow.

Frank was starting to get more concerned. He finally decided to go on to Italy hoping that if the investigation revealed anything they wouldn't be able to find him, or at least not for a long, long time. While checking into flights, Frank thought he might as well check into another country to go to just in case he needed it. *Even though the weather isn't ideal, Zurich, Switzerland may be a good place to hide out. Think I'll check into getting multiple flights while I'm at it, so I'll be ready to move on. Toronto may be a good place as well. I'll just investigate those places before I make my decision. It shouldn't take too long. That way I can stay in Cancun a little while longer. This place is terrific,* Frank thought.

CHAPTER 23

As Redmond entered the precinct, he noticed Brower on the phone. He poured himself a cup of coffee and grabbed a donut off Brower's desk.

"Sure thing, guys, we'll be right there," Brower responded.

"Come on, Redmond, the lab has some answers for us."

"What time did you get here Brower? I was surprised to see you busy at work already."

"I couldn't sleep much so I came in at 6 a.m. and started going over what little bit of evidence there is, which isn't much for working on this case as long as we have. I hope the lab has some revealing evidence."

As they walked into the lab, Mark, the lab technician, had a smile on his face.

"Glad you boys could come down here so quickly. You

are going to be singing my praises for a while! Well, here is your report, but I'll just fill you in on my findings. The bottle and pill you brought in from the Callahan house is arsenic. And when I figured that out, I knew you'd want to know about the white powder-like stuff on the bottom of your shoe, Brower. So, I finished processing that as well and that one is meth."

"Hey Redmond, I think we just hit not one but two jackpots!" Brower exclaimed.

"Thanks Mark, we owe you big time for this!"

They high fived each other as they were leaving.

They were laughing and talking on their way back to their office, so excited with the latest outcome. They ran into the detective who was looking into all the deaths that had been happening in their city.

"Hey Rich, how's your investigation going?" asked Brower. "I think yours has been going on longer than ours, hasn't it?"

"Yes, I've got some good leads, but just can't seem to get a break in the case."

They all went back to Brower's office, and they discussed both of their cases and wondered if there was any connection between the two. Wanting to have all their facts together, they spent the next three days piecing everything together until they had both cases pretty much solved.

But they couldn't figure out what Frank's motive was in killing Henry. In the meantime, Redmond had a couple of guys checking on flights and transportation out of town for Frank, and they finally tracked him to Cancun. After contacting authorities there, they looked at video footage at the airport on the day he arrived and tracked him to the place where he was staying. After showing his picture around, someone recognized him and said that he'd lost a lot of weight and gave the authorities a description of him. They found out he had checked out that morning. At the airport, viewing security footage, they found Frank had taken a flight to London. Because the flight was around 13 hours, they had some time to prepare to send the authorities to meet him when he got off the plane. Now that Brower and Redmond had everything under control with Frank, it was time to go to Justice Medical.

Upon arriving with several officers and warrants in hand, Bob, Sabrina, Brock, Gary, and Harold were arrested. While interrogating Bob, the investigators learned that *Milagro* was the brainchild of Frank. He wanted a quick way to make money so he could retire, hoping it would take off if placed in crucial places. Bob was the second in charge to carry out the plan. Sabrina was hired as the sales representative when she arrived but wasn't aware of the plan until she and Bob had an affair a year after she was there. Then she and Bob realized that they could make a lot of money if they combined forces against Frank. Brock was used as leverage and because he was so willing to do anything they asked, they were able to use him to their advantage. Brock was stunned when he found out what Frank, Bob, and Sabrina had done. The police realized he was innocent in the whole scheme of things and released him. Gary and Harold were charged with making meth with intent to distribute which was used in the making of *Milagro*. Bob and Sabrina were charged as co-conspirators with making, possession, intent to distribute meth, along with several other charges. Frank was arrested in London and transported back to Nashville. All the while insisting he hadn't done anything wrong. After being delivered to the precinct and interrogated by Detectives Brower and Redmond, Frank finally confessed to Henry's death and being the instigator of *Milagro*.

"I knew Henry was dying, but I was planning to buy him out and take over the company, I guess I was a little too eager to get my hands on the company," Frank said.

"So, you're telling me greed was what caused you to poison Henry?" Brower said.

"Yes, I guess it was," replied Frank.

After combining all the information, they realized that the *Milagro* was causing people to get addicted to meth, an ingredient in the capsule. As a result they died from an overdose because of the overuse of the weight loss system. Frank had figured that putting a little meth in the mixture would ensure an addiction so he could sell a lot of *Milagro*.

He didn't think it would be enough to kill people. But he wasn't anticipating the overuse of the capsule they created. Detectives Rich, Brower, and Redmond decided they had enough evidence to make arrests in both cases. Frank, Bob, and Sabrina were also charged with the deaths of six people, and the families of the deceased sued Justice Medical.

After Brock's arrest and release, he wanted to see Janice. While driving there he wanted to see if there was any calming music on the radio, which he needed badly because of the day he had. He turned it on and just as he did, he heard, "We have breaking news on WHOW." He turned the radio off. After arriving at Janice's house and telling her the whole sordid story, she was shocked and was concerned for Brock's well-being, although in her heart she was glad he didn't have that particular job anymore. He had changed so much while there. Brock told Janice he'd had enough excitement the past few days and needed to go home to get some rest. While driving home, he turned on the radio to see if he could find some worship music. It had been a while since he'd listened to it. He had strayed away from the life he had while growing up in Ohio. As he was changing the station, he heard an announcer on the radio say, "We have an update for you on the deaths in the city, and an exclusive report on another breaking story. We'll let you know more about these stories at the 6 p.m. hour. This is Jerry Rhodes reporting for WHOW."

Brock shook his head and wondered how he didn't see something wrong at Justice. How had he been deceived again, or were they just that good at lying that he wasn't aware of the deception in which he was involved? *I can't believe Sabrina was so involved in this mess. Someday maybe I can talk with her and hear her side. I should have listened to Janice, but I guess I was so enthralled with making money and success I didn't see it. I better call my parents to let them know before they hear it on the news. Better still, I think I'll go see them since it's been a while.* After arriving home, he checked out flights and found one leaving at 6 a.m. He booked it and called his parents to let them know he was coming. They were thrilled to know he was coming for a visit. *I hope it won't upset them too much, but they need to hear the story in person rather than on the phone or on the TV if it becomes national news.* Brock called Janice to let her know his plans and then went straight to bed after he booked his flight, mentally and emotionally exhausted after the past several days.

During the flight the next morning, Brock reminisced about his days in Ohio. His friends had all moved to other states and had successful jobs. He would be happy to see his parents again and his hometown. After renting a car, he drove to his childhood home. His parents saw him drive up and ran outside to see him. It made him think of the story of the prodigal son in the Bible. A story he hadn't thought of in a long time. He settled in to spend a week there. After telling his parents the whole story about his relationship with Carrie and why he'd gone to Nashville in the first place, he told them about his job at Justice Medical and his relationship with Sabrina and how everything came to an end. They were sympathetic to his situation. The offer of comfort and not judgment was part of who they were as people and parents. They always offered grace to everyone. It was wonderful being there, but he knew he needed to get back to Nashville. He loved that town, even though it had brought him hardship. He missed his friend Janice and told his parents about her and the friendship they had and how much encouragement and support she'd offered him. As the week came to a close, he hugged and kissed his parents goodbye. They enjoyed his time there so much. While driving away he looked back at them, and he saw his mother wipe a tear away. He had tears in his eyes as well. It had been too long since he'd visited them.

After a few days back in Nashville, he received a call from Sabrina's attorney. He informed Brock that he was listed as a beneficiary to Justice Medical. Since Sabrina and Bob were going to prison, they needed someone to run the business. Brock was stunned. He didn't know what he should do, so he called his parents and Janice to tell them and have them pray over his decision about running the company. So many lives and jobs were at stake. He also needed to talk with Sabrina. After a couple of days of deliberation, he decided to see Sabrina to hear her side of the story. Brock wanted to do the right thing, but there was so much at risk and so much involved; he wasn't sure that he was qualified to run the company. Sabrina understood Brock's position. Justice Medical had suffered a major setback. He wasn't sure it could overcome the obstacles to continue making *Milagro*. The fraudulent venture at Justice Medical turned out to be the end of a very profitable company. Because of the lawsuits, they had decided to file bankruptcy then to close the company. Many lives were devastated because of the closure, but because of the circumstances, they all understood. It was a grief they all shared.

Brock decided he wouldn't have to return to work right away. *Maybe in a couple of weeks or so I'll start looking,* Brock thought. *Think I'll just give myself some time to heal after this tragedy.* That evening his phone rang.

"Hey Brock, it's Janice. It's Friday night. You want to go to The Grill? Maybe take your guitar in case you decide to sing?"

They both laughed and decided to go.

"Maybe you'll get 'the big break' and you'll be able to start a new career!" Janice told him.